GW01043917

Inspec

and the

Winter Wolf

S Kellow Bingham

Other books coming soon in the series:

Inspector Bassé and the Lost Boys
Inspector Bassé and the Heatwave
Inspector Bassé and the Revenant
Inspector Bassé and the Long Shadow

Inspector Bassé and the Winter Wolf

S Kellow Bingham

Prologue.

One, two, three, breathe, four, five, six.

What do I know of anger? What can I tell of such dainty feelings as simmering outrage? That anger is fear. That it is a civilised and nuanced reaction to the horrors of this life. That anger is a luxury in the face of raw fury, a rage that would tear down every thread of civilization and expose the rotten flesh of corruption at its heart.

Childhood storms of wrath tore me from my home and led darkly into either forest or city wasteland, where I would awake naked with dirt in my mouth and blood beneath my fingernails. Moments fuelled by such powerful currents I thought they might kill me. Dreams of wild orgies of destruction took time and patience for me to understand.

At last, time and patience spent by my mother and grandfather meant these furies died down, then became something else, an energy controlled by will. My father, the illusionist, taught me to train, to control the savage beast within. I remember the force behind the emotion, the taste of dirt, the scent of wild creatures deep in the forest, the sound of rain dripping through trees, and the darkness.

I would lie with my animal self, exhausted.

I never dared believe it could happen again, but here I am streaked in mud and blood deep in the woods. Dawn light picks out bare Winter trees. I should be freezing without my clothes, but I feel blood coursing through my dark interior like another heart is beating there, keeping me warm.

It can't last. My mother and grandfather are no longer here to protect me. My father a phantom. I have to do this on my own. Dark scars cut deep through the snow. It's my way out of the forest and back to a civilized world, out of the fury that drove me here, back to small irritations and mild outrages of daily life. I follow tracks made by a monster I don't remember, that must have been here, but thankfully is no longer.

The sky lightens. It will be a clear morning. The first rays of the sun pick out ice hanging from tree branches. I need boots. I need a coat, and I need not to be seen in this condition.

Chapter One.

Old thoughts ran through my head as my train drew into the station at Bayeux. It's been ten years since I was here last. I left for Paris in 1879. Since then, so much has changed, I wondered whether I was returning to the same city I left.

Letters I received in Guyana told me little. Father had disappeared. A lost love had another baby. My appointment and promotion to Inspector had been approved. What was I coming home to? What was I coming home for? What did I expect? Is Bayeux home anymore?

I remember the frozen icy water of the river Aure from my very first year here in the city, marvelling at how small Bayeux was after growing up in Paris. But the river will not reveal its secrets on my command. The ice will remain closed to my demands.

I was twelve years old and late for school, so I took a shortcut across the river below the weir. My new friends and I decided the ice must have been solid enough to take a coach and horses. Halfway across I caught my foot on something and fell flat on my face, the breath was knocked out of me. As I lay gasping like a fish, I spotted a murky thing beneath the ice, gradually rising to the surface.

Ice creaked and popped as the river continued to flow beneath it, where the living water had been coerced into culverts and canals, through mills and bridges for centuries in the heart of the city of Bayeux. The natural course of the river is contained by a will greater than its savage soul. It is made to feed and power the porcelain and tanning industries that line its banks and carry its secrets out to the sea.

But secrets are stubborn. Some are held back by the winter ice. The thaw may come early and release these confidences to the sea, but sometimes that hidden savagery can rise to the surface, determined to be discovered.

The thing was dark and was wrapped in sacking. I waited a moment, curiosity greater than fear. It bumped up against the

6

ice and began to rotate. The sacking caught on the ice and began to peel back revealing cold white skin. A face appeared, the eyes sightless. I leapt up and ran as fast as I could and arrived at the school gates with moments to spare.

I felt my fury rise. The skin on my arms prickled and my blood ran hot, but I had learned to channel and contain my rage at the injustice in the world. My will was stronger than the animal that lived inside me. The natural force had to be held back if I was to live a civilized life.

I didn't tell anyone. Who would believe I saw a dead man in the river on his final journey? I read the local newspaper and went as far as visiting the Commissariat, the police headquarters, to read their notices of missing persons. Nothing. As soon as I was old enough, I signed up as a police cadet. The river Aure held secrets. It spirited them away. One day I swore I would find out where they came from. I would not ignore them.

But I shook these nonsense thoughts from my head. I was here because I have a job to do. It's my duty to take charge of the Commissariat and serve the people, with no mind to my own difficulties.

The porter was on the platform with my trunk. I tipped him and it was removed to the hotel. It's taken almost a month to arrive here, sailing from the tropics, past Devil's Island penitentiary then along the American coast, across the Atlantic. Cherbourg to Bayeux was the least of it, the railway still looked brand new.

The weather was biting cold. It will take some getting used to.

*

'I thought they were sending you to South America?' Sergeant Royer did not look up from his ledger. 'Was the Southern hemisphere not to your liking?'

I was impressed that after all these years I was still remembered. In fact, Royer's banter felt almost welcome.

'I liked it well enough Sergeant,' I said. 'I almost married.'

Royer laughed, a hoarse roar I was well familiar with. His moustache quivered in the middle of his ruddy face, and spittle flew onto his book. It seemed nothing much had changed, and the years fell away. But I was no longer the new recruit, terrified of this man's rustic authority.

'A born escapologist Bassé,' chuckled Royer, 'just like our old commissaire. So why are you back in Bayeux? Come to see how well we've all aged? Out to lift my pension at the card table?'

'Indeed Sergeant, both,' I said as I fished in my jacket for an envelope, which was addressed to Commissaire Hautefort. I handed Royer the letter, which was my winning hand. My best poker face set.

'What's this?' He said, inspecting the typed address. 'You know old Hautefort retired at last? Even so, he still comes in from time to time.'

'It is my letter of appointment for the files,' I said, 'addressed to Commissaire Hautefort out of protocol. You know how these things work.'

Royer nodded and slit the envelope open with a silver letter opener. Nothing happened without following due process. This was the state's greatest strength and her ultimate weakness. He pulled out the letter, carefully set it on the desk and began to read to himself in his slow deliberate manner, lips quivering as he silently mouthed the words. I watched with some satisfaction as his eyes widened.

'Congratulations sir,' he said at last and raised his hand in a salute. 'I trust you know the way to your office Commissaire?'

'Indeed, I do Sergeant,' I returned his salute and then extended my hand, 'and I very much look forward to working with you once more.'

'Thank you, sir,' Royer pumped my hand a little too long. I watched with some satisfaction as his face twitched while he took in the new situation.

I climbed the staircase at the back of the building. It opened onto a long corridor that ran through the middle of the Commissariat from end to end. I stopped at the top of the stairs and paused for a moment to let it all sink in. The smell of old polished wood, mouldering files, tobacco, and burned coffee. I had started my career in police work right here in this building. In those days Sergeant Royer had been my superior, by turns encouraging and terrifying. He taught me my first lessons in policing, in paperwork, and how to get things done. How to sniff out a liar and when to call off a chase. The basics, good strong stuff.

The training meant it was impossible to walk down a street without anticipating some lawless action that might be taking place behind closed doors and quietly curtained windows. A good policeman is always observing, forever on the lookout, for criminality is everywhere. Most people, I imagine, lead blissful lives completely unaware of the number of cutthroats and charlatans, shapeshifters and monsters who walk the streets mimicking respectability, passing as law-abiding creatures. If they knew what we knew, they would likely stay indoors petitioning the authorities to have them hunted down and removed to Devil's Island. But we are as visible to rogues as they are to the police, having had their apprenticeship on the other side of the law. They wait for us to be looking in the wrong direction while we wait for them to make their mistakes.

My new office was at one end of the landing, with shuttered windows that gave out over the Rue Royale. From here there is a view of the entire market square and the flags that top the office of the mayor. There's also a partial view of the Western façade of the famous cathedral, with its high green dome dominating the sky.

The old house also faces the same direction but onto the market square, opposite the commercial side, built as a challenge to the world by my father. He styled the house like a chateau with a turret and a gated forecourt. He believed us descended from a mix of Transylvanian and Arabian royalty. There is nothing wrong with imagination, but I find the facts of life to be far more complicated than any extraordinary illusion conjured by an old magician. I love my father and his fantasies, but I am a man of hard reality, with no mind for magic.

The office felt somewhat grandiose. In Paris, I shared an office with a dozen other men. In Cayenne, the capital city of French Guyana, I shared with lizards, parrots, snakes, and many-coloured frogs. I could not say which I preferred, and just now, either place seems a long way off.

They tell you that you can never go backwards, and that life is a process of always moving forward. It is true. I have returned to Bayeux, but it has changed and so have I. It's not the city I left behind. I am not the same man who departed for Paris looking for promotion and other excitements. I've had my fill of adventure in this lifetime. I'm looking forward to the certain, dull nature of local small-city crime.

Hautefort's old desk sat heavy with dust, the room abandoned and unused for some time. The curtains were yellow with pipe smoke and age. It felt a lot like home. The last time I'd been in here, standing in this office, was when I shook Inspector Hautefort's hand before I left for Paris. My mind conjured the scene and I saw a hint of sadness, and perhaps relief in his eyes. Most likely that was simply my fancy. Like Royer, the old inspector had never been a sentimental man.

There was a knock at the door. It was Sergeant Royer.

'I will send in the housekeeper Inspector,' he said. 'I do apologise, it has been a while and so we were not expecting, that is to say, we have been sailing without a captain for a little while now.'

'Understandable,' I said, 'I only received confirmation very recently myself.'

Royer looked relieved. He's not a bad policeman. God knows there are worse in Paris. He'd been tough on me when I started out, but he was the same with all the new men. I couldn't count it against him.

'Do we have any business I should know about?' I said. 'Are there any interesting guests in our donjon?'

'No sir,' he shrugged, 'just the usual old faces. We had a dead man in the morgue. He was found drowned in the river. Bloated like a pig he was, a terrible smell. He reminded me of that whale washed up at Luc-sur-Mer in 'eighty-five. My wife made me take her on the train to go and see the poor dead thing. My God, I swear you could almost smell it from Bayeux when the wind was in the North. Well, this man, God rest him and forgive me for saying so, he smelled almost as bad as the whale.'

'Are we certain it was a drowning?' I said, ignoring Royer's exaggerations.

'Yes sir, just like I said sir,' Royer scratched his chin, 'bad business. Not a nice way to go, but I reckon it would have been quick, what with it being so cold of late.'

'Who was he?'

'Sorry sir, I don't recall.'

'You know perfectly well Royer,' I said, 'I remember your memory for detail. It terrified me when I was a cadet, and it would be a tragedy if it had dimmed since we last spoke. You used to tell me to notice everything and forget nothing.'

'I apologise Commissaire,' said Royer, 'perhaps you are right, and my faculties are simply ageing without me realising?'

'I am going out for lunch,' I gave the sergeant a look that let him know I did not believe a word, 'when I return, I would like to see the case file on my desk and dossiers for all personnel. I would like to see how well Bayeux is manned these days.'

'Very good sir,'

I marched past the sergeant, crossed the landing, and clattered down the stairs. The commissariat felt a little too quiet, slumbering under the dust of ages past. There are a thousand years of history in this city, each one a page inked with familiar tales. It's time for some new stories, time to shake off the dust and bring the city's police force into the modern age.

Constable Mouche was on the front desk for Royer. They joined up together more than thirty years ago. His moustache had silvered too, but otherwise he looked the same as when I left.

'Good day Constable,' I said as I passed.

'Good day to you too sir,' said Mouche. The news was already circulating. I would call a meeting later in the day and address the men. Right then, I was far too hungry to do anything sensible.

11

Across the street, as I walked out of the building was the Café du Guillaume. I took a seat at the junction at the East end of the Rue Royale. From here I had a view all the way across the Market Square. I used to walk past the Commissariat every day. The old house was just a hundred paces North. A step too far for today.

It was cold and my breath clouded in front of my face. The waiter, old and wrapped up in a coat and scarf against the January chill, staggered over to where I sat. The weak sun had climbed as high as it'd go and sent down a poor pale light into the market square.

I ordered a coffee and watched the townspeople out and about on their business. I searched their faces for any clue of remembrance. Many had the familiar cast of the region, all a little paler, all a centimetre or two taller than the milieu I left behind. All of them, every single one, look like people I once knew.

The coffee was good, dark, and strong, the way I like it. The coffee in Cayenne was rich and fruity, with a forceful, almost overpowering chocolate bitterness. I'd not found its flavour replicated anywhere else, but Guillaume's coffee was good enough. I sipped and watched and thought and sipped.

I ordered the plat du jour, it was a cassoulet, good, thick fare for a cold day. I dipped my bread and sipped a cold glass of water. There was no need to hurry. Not today.

After an hour or so I returned to my new office and was pleased to see the window reflected in the walnut desktop. The housekeeper had left the windows ajar, and a light breeze was gently clearing the old stale air left behind by other lungs. In the middle of the desk was the file that I supposed held the report on the drowned man. Next to it were two stacks of dossiers detailing the staff under my command. Next to them was a fresh pile of paperwork, the blood of the police force, the stuff that kept everything, the nation, La France, moving forward.

In a chaotic world, I enjoyed the steadfast regularity of paperwork. Whatever happens in France one can always rely on the bureaucracy of state business to remain. Without this

12

steadfast order, chaos would rule the day. Sometimes it felt like the gendarmerie was the last bastion of civilization in a cruel battle, but as long as this massive bulwark of administration held, our great nation would overcome any headwind.

I picked up the case file. It had the name of Deputy Inspector Didier Ouimet on the front. I had yet to meet him. Inside, the report was a thin affair and I saw at once Royer's sin of omission. The dead man's name was Jean Mortain. The address was one I knew well. I had spent much of my youth getting in and out of trouble, in and out of church and school, with Jean Mortain.

I read the scant details of his fate, of his discovery one cold morning, face down in the frozen reeds on the banks of the Aure. His body had been trapped by the ice built up at the old bridge at the end of the Rue Tire-Vit. It was not a road name to be found on any map, but it was well known in the city for its particular attraction for a certain clientele. Jean had been found by a rough-house barkeeper on her way to market one morning.

The last time I saw him Jean had been passed out from drinking on the floor of his kitchen. We'd been having a final evening of cards and wine before I left for Paris. It did not matter who won or lost that night. It'd been an evening of laughing and promises, of two young men trying to make sense of where they were and what was happening in a world that neither recognized anymore. From here it seemed a very long time ago.

I closed the file and pushed back my chair, closed my eyes. This was devastating news. I felt my heart begin to race and a warmth filled my arms and legs. One, two three, counting my breath, four, five, six, the heat began to recede, and my heart seemed to slow. A civilised response to tragic news. A gentleman of the law is calm in the face of grief. He understands but does not indulge in the raw emotions, for they are potentially injurious.

I'd been looking forward to reacquainting myself with old friends, reminiscing and catching up, perhaps finding some

13

meaning in returning to the old place. It was one of the reasons I applied to fill this post. I wanted to come home to Bayeux. I had wanted my travels and experience to mean something to someone at last. God knows I'd made friends in Paris, and then later in the colonies, but not where I'd expected to. Perhaps coming home was a mistake? But I'm here now. Too late for Jean. Too late for my father too. Hopefully in time for the rest of my friends, and for myself.

Home. I still had not gone as far as to think seriously about visiting the house my father had abandoned when he disappeared with his new wife. What should I think of him and my youthful stepmother? I shook my head. Clotilde had been a sincere bride, from her letters of that I was certain, but I always retained a nervous regard for the match. I received the keys to the house from the family Notaire, and another small stack of letters, but the particular pleasure of revisiting and deciding what to do with the place would have to wait.

I took up the stack of dossiers relating to the men under my command. Royer's was thin for a man so long served, but he was someone who preferred to keep things brief and to the point. More interesting was my Deputy, Didier Ouimet, up from Laval in the Mayenne. Was he looking to return home too or was he searching for something, like I had been? I shook my head. Measuring others by one's own gauge never worked, but I would like to understand his story.

The rest were a mixed troop of gentlemen, some scholars but most were local soldiery looking to serve their own. I hoped they would come to realise that I was as local as they were, despite appearances. I recognised one or two names. There had been a Leverrier in the school choir, a sergeant now, and the name Desnier was familiar too. I seemed to remember arresting a Desnier, a wolf in man's clothing, many years ago before I left town.

I finished my survey and slipped quietly out of the commissariat. It was still not yet three in the afternoon. I knew the way to Jean's house, and let my legs take me the well-remembered route, down the Rue Royale, away from the old house. I wasn't ready to walk by it just yet.

14

When I arrived at the end of the street, I caught the overwhelming aroma of sardines being grilled. The scent, laid on a bed of frosty air, started my stomach off on a cry for sustenance. I quietly scolded it for blasphemy. Supper could wait.

I rapped on Mortain's door once, twice, three times. My shoulders dropped. There was nobody home, but as I turned away, I heard an old woman call out.

'What do you want? You make enough noise to raise the dead.'

'If only I could,' I thought to myself. I looked up. The woman was wearing an old-fashioned bonnet. It was the kind I remember my mother swearing she would never wear. The crone leaned out over the sill of a second-storey window, the casement was webby and cracked with age.

'I'll not come downstairs for you,' she said, 'tell me your business. Why are you breaking down my door?'

'My apologies madame,' I raised my hat to her. 'I come looking for an old friend, the monsieur Jean Mortain. We were in school together.'

'He was at Baartram the undertaker last night,' she said, 'but you will have to be quick as they're taking him to the cemetery at first light tomorrow morning.'

'Thank you, madame,' I touched my hat once more and made off back down the street. A hasty funeral then, no doubt due to the poor condition of my friend.

I arrived at the undertaker's establishment as the cold winter light was starting to fade. I hoped there would be few other customers. I walked around to the side of the building to the yard where they readied the horses and found a boy who would fetch me his master. After a short wait, a man appeared in a suit that looked older than Napoleon. It was as black as iron while his face was as white as that of a dead man.

'Yes sir?' he said, 'Can I help you?'

'Inspector Bassé,' I said, 'Bayeux Gendarmerie. I need to see Jean Mortain.'

The old gentleman's face appeared to leach even more colour. I wondered for a moment how old Baartram might be. Was he one of the deathless, the vampire people that live for the blood of the battlefield? I shook my head, surely there was no longer a place for their kind in modern France.

'Come in sir,' he said, 'I am afraid monsieur Mortain is in a closed coffin and not fit to be seen.'

'I understand.' I watched the undertaker's walk. He was as old and rheumatic as he looked.

'He is in the chapel with his wife and family at the moment. If you wish I will ask if they would mind you paying your respects.'

'That will not be necessary. Will they be here long?'

'Who sir?'

'The family?'

'Ah, I see,' the old undertaker scratched at the papery skin under his chin, 'this is business and not personal. No sir, I do not believe they will be long as we have concluded our dealings as far as we can for the moment.'

'Good, then please ask them all to leave as you have other urgent affairs to attend to,' I said, 'official state matters, administration, reports, you know what I mean, and please, do not mention that I am here. I do not wish to make their suffering the worse.'

'I think I understand you sir, but if you will permit me to ask, what state matters would that be sir?' he continued to rub at his chin.

'I need you to open the coffin,' I said.

'But sir?'

'Yes, I am aware that it will not be pretty, but believe me I would rather not waste another minute.' I said, holding his watery gaze.

'Have you a letter of authorization from the magistrate?'

'I confess I do not, however, if you would rather wait until after tomorrow's funeral to open the coffin then so be it, but we will have wasted time and rather stepped off on the wrong foot sir.'

The old gentleman weighed my words for a moment. 'Very well sir,' he said, 'we should be closing for the day soon anyway.'

16

'Thank you,' I said.

'And if we wait much longer then the work will be that much more difficult.'

'Time waits for no man Baartram.'

'I am very well aware of that Inspector.'

'Of course,' I hid my smile as I followed Monsieur Baartram into the dark internal space of his establishment. I was made to wait behind a purpose-made carved rood screen that reflected themes and figures inscribed on similar pieces in the cathedral. The undertaker made discreet noises to his clients about his business. He had a peculiar warmth mixed with a solemnity that seemed to be a hallmark of all good men of his profession. Likewise, I have seldom met a miserable butcher.

I studied Jean's widow, Marie. Her fine and beautiful face was a portrait of true and intense grief. I had not seen her for many years and yet, even under these terrible circumstances, she had not lost the beauty that I remembered. She held two small children close to her. Besides this trio were a couple I recognized as her parents, although they had aged far more than seemed possible. Jean's parents were likely either dead or too elderly to make anything other than essential journeys. I imagined Jean had taken over the family shop. What would become of it? Would Marie be its keeper now?

Marie Daufresne had once been the target of my affections. But in those days, many years ago, I'd lacked the confidence that Jean had with women. As time passed, however, Jean became more wedded to the bottle than to Marie.

My father's ambition also counted against any idea that Marie might be for me. He had a singular plan that I should be raised as a gentleman and despite Mme Daufresne's beauty, she remained a lowly paysan's daughter. I was destined for greater things. His illusion was that I should become a gentleman alchemist or some such, a man with position. A scientist, a discoverer of new knowledge. He was much taken with the Englishman, Darwin. For my part, I craved the invisibility that comes with the wearing of a uniform. The certainty that I should not stand out in a world where difference, while not a crime, had its disadvantages.

17

To my father's dismay, as soon as I finished my schooling, I started with the Bayeux Gendarmerie, having applied in secret, and been accepted. I signed the contract and moved into the barracks on the same day. A fait accompli. Permission would never have been forthcoming from my father, and as the old saying goes, sometimes it is better to ask for forgiveness.

It was never mentioned.

By then Jean and Marie had been promised to each other, but it was too late for either of them. The promise could not be kept. Marie and I had broken it on the many occasions that Jean had been in his cups, maintaining his other promise to the goddess of the wine bottle.

I watched her leave the undertaker's chapel with her children and her parents. I felt a little of my heartbreak and then scolded myself. A bleak anger rose up inside me. What did I expect? That everything would be the same? That I would slip back into my old life like no time had passed at all? I would be back at the card table with Jean, waiting for him to pass out so that I could rekindle the passion I shared with Marie. Pretending I was in control, beating a man at cards then making a mistress of his wife.

Love without consequences, friendship without commitment. It was one of the things that had made me run to Paris in the first place, this strange, displaced passion, but it had not been far enough. There were express trains these days that could bring a body back across the country at an unholy eighty kilometres an hour. Towns and villages flashed past and suddenly you were back where you started.

No. It was better to leave for somewhere so remote the modern world could never reach it in so short a time. It was what was required. South America took me and changed me. Time passed, and now here I was in an undertaker's office. The world and my friends had changed too.

One, two, three, breathe, four, five, six.

Chapter Two.

I waited behind the screen until the undertaker Baartram returned from showing out the family. He carried a brace and bit with which to un-turn the screws that secured the lid of Mortain's coffin. He had a thin stick of a boy in tow carrying a pail full of rags. I came out from the hiding place to meet them.

'Thank you Baartram,' I said.

'Quite alright sir,' he said.

He took up his mechanical screwdriver and began unwinding the brass screws. His boy squeezed the rags out into the holes and wiped around the lid of the box. The boy was nearly as tall as the undertaker and as pale. His hair was an ice-white blond, and his eyes were grey too, making him seem almost ghost-like. The pair moved with a slow deliberation, borne of long hours working together. I thought again of the Deathless ones. How Napoleon had exiled any that had once been servants of the crown, or the state. Rumours whispered that they were still among us, that all the creatures that weren't desirable, were still here, hiding, waiting, surviving out of sight.

I prefer not to think about such things. I believe only in what I can see. I am the son of an illusionist. Only that which is real, and actual interests me.

'We had to seal the top with joiner's glue,' explained Baartram, 'but the work was only done this morning so it will still be soft enough to yield. We make it ourselves in our workshop with fresh bones from the butcher. Fresh once a week and the best quality. Good as any you might see in your fancy workshops in Paris.'

'I don't doubt it,' I said.

'I am very much afraid that you will be able to smell the gentleman soon,' said Baartram, 'so you may require your handkerchief.'

I heard a short gasp of escaping air as the seal was broken on the top half of the lid. It was like the out-breath after a punch to the stomach. I covered my nose and mouth as instructed and waited. Baartram and his boy set aside the lid and stepped a good distance away.

'We did the best we could for the gentleman sir,' he said, his face expressing a mix of regret, disappointment, and horror.

I nodded my thanks, not wanting to take the cloth from my face. No time to breathe. I peered into the coffin. The shroud cloth was stained. I leaned over and pulled back a dry corner. The cloth stuck to the body in several places, but I had to see. His face was a mess, but it was that of my old friend Jean.

Poor Mortain. He was in a state of decomposition hastened by submersion in the river Aure and had been underwater for some time. I imagined him being tangled in tree roots or fishing lines before being dislodged and floating to the surface. Had he not been caught somewhere then I was certain he would have been out to sea by now. I had seen similar corpses pulled from the Seine in Paris. The Maroni in Guyana was less forgiving, it teemed with flesh-eating fish, leaving little for anyone to bury. Often just a few bones, held together with ligaments and gristle, were all that remained.

It was clear where Baartram had done his best to tidy Mortain for his final journey, but he was not a bag of corn to be stitched up. I moved to the other end and raised the cloth over his feet. Toenails were missing, consistent with the circumstances, however, a closer inspection revealed regular indentations over each ankle. Possible rope marks I wondered? It was hard to say for certain, the skin was broken, and the calf was puffed out and swollen.

I checked his right wrist, arm, and hand. His index finger was missing. A clean cut, which might be something or nothing in this situation. Perhaps a knife, maybe a rat? Suddenly my old friend was simply a victim with a list of marks and features that deserved some small scrutiny, but there were few clues left that had not been muddied by the waters. I saw little point in recording any observations in my notebook, there was too little to signify the cause of death other than drowning. I signalled to Baartram that he could re-seal the coffin.

*

Walking away from the undertaker's in the growing dark I considered whether I should pay a visit to the old house tonight. I knew it was empty and had been for almost five years since my father's disappearing act with his new wife, Clotilde. I would need the place cleaned before I could even think about moving in. Not to mention how cold it would be, and that I should engage a housekeeper.

It was a fine strategy, filling my head with these thoughts to keep my grief at bay. I had lost a good friend, and the world would no longer be the same. Before today I had the comfort of knowing that even though my family was no more, my friends would be constant. Now that prop had been taken away. Nothing was cast in stone.

I went directly to the Hotel de Ville where my trunk had been delivered to a room. As far as I knew, thanks to correspondence received from Inspector Hautefort, this was where my father and his wife were last seen. One night they were here, the next morning they were gone. No one saw them leave. A vanishing act.

It's tempting to think my father might have re-joined the travelling show to live out his final years on the road to Moscow, St Petersburg, Constantinople, or Athens. However, he displayed little nostalgia for that way of life and appeared to have grown comfortable in Bayeux. Then he met his new wife while I was away in Guyana. What happened next remains a mystery. One I'm determined to get to the bottom of.

At the hotel, I set the concierge to deliver hands to open up the old house. I would inspect following the funeral tomorrow and meet with a recommended housekeeper. In the hotel's restaurant, I was restored with a fine winter soup after which I settled on amusing myself with card tricks.

*

I returned to the undertakers before first light. I'd not slept well. There were too many questions, far too much I could not hope to know. Jean and my father had populated my dreams, teasing me with their secrets. Baartram was all ready and waiting in the mews, his horse and carriage immaculate. The coffin was on board, so I took up a place next to the horses and waited.

As the sky began to lighten from the deepest blue-black to the palest grey, I could see figures begin to approach the cortege from each end of the street. I spotted Marie Daufresne straight away. She was veiled and walked with a controlled grace at the head of a small family group. A little behind I could see Dufy and Reynard, old friends, old school choirboys, and card players both. I felt a lump rise in my throat. This was not the reunion I had envisaged while I waited out the days crossing the Atlantic. I kept my head down, not wanting to catch the eye or distract from the carriage.

As the procession moved off, I stayed in front with the horses. I could quite easily have been taken for one of Baartram's men. In this moment I was less interested in who may be following the coffin. Experience has borne out some remarkably peculiar laws of attraction concerning crime. Most criminals will return to a scene of a transgression without thought or motivation simply because it is close to home or near their place of work. In truth, it is for the most part, unavoidable. Then there are the mischief makers who delight in the disruption and confusion they cause and will not be happy until they see the ripples their action has caused, and the effect they have had on the rest of the world. Besides them, there are still others who like to think of themselves as more capable than law enforcement and play at cat and mouse games. To be fair, in my experience, there are any number of policemen who would struggle to find their boots, let alone discover the identity of a determined criminal.

A perpetrator of an offence who has used a particular method with some success will most likely tend to repeat themselves, sometimes blow by blow. Other crimes, by their very execution, will bear all the hallmarks of a directed piece of work. If Jean Mortain's murderer was either a first-timer or a professional, I doubted that either would be able to resist the

22

pull of the cortege. I watched each alleyway, every doorway, as we passed by, parading their work through the streets of the city.

The sky had lost its dawn silver and had become an ice-cold blue. Wisps of pale clouds decorated the heavens like lost feathers. A perfect morning for a funeral, spoiled only by a raucous early morning seagull chorus serenading us from the rooftops.

Old ladies pushed open their shutters and gazed down at us from first-floor windows. A butcher's boy propped his bicycle on the wall and doffed his cap. At his feet was a small dog, a terrier, giving the boy's basket an unbroken stare.

All the boulanger's doors were open to the day, filling the streets of the city with their reassuring aromas. Someone was smoking rough tobacco, and I became aware of the immediate warm smell of the horses and their polished leathers. I caught woodsmoke, coal, and lamp oil in the air. I let go of the horse and stepped quietly to the side, and let the slow procession pass me by, watching in the reflection of a butcher's shop window.

The cemetery at Bayeux is like all the others I have ever seen in France or her dominions, a broad mix of the grand and the humble. Some are housed better in death than they were in life. Mortain fell somewhere near the bottom of the scale. He would have a temporary plaque that was likely to remain his permanent memorial.

The lowest order, the beasts, were interred beyond the wall, outside of sacred ground, apart from human society. They may have passed amongst us while alive, but in death, those lies are always exposed. I'm not sure I agree. It doesn't sit right with me, but then, most monsters I meet are well and truly human.

There was a corner of this place set aside for me by my grandpa. He expected us all to join him eventually so invested in a good size plot with a view of the road leading out of town. 'It's not for the Tsars, it is for us, and it will do.' He said at the time.

He was a very proud man. His parents had been buried thousands of miles away and hundreds of miles apart. My mother is here, buried next to him.

I watched at the back of the group of mourners as my old friend made his final journey into the earth. I could be wrong. The Jean Mortain I knew was a drunk after all. It could have been a terrible accident and nothing more.

When the graveside ritual was over, I remained where I was as the mourners left. Marie Daufresne stopped beside me and pushed her children ahead into the arms of their grandparents.

'I knew it was you straight away. I thought perhaps you must be a ghost,' she whispered, 'we were so sure you were dead and buried by now.'

'I am so sorry Marie.'

'Don't,' she took a step away, then changed her mind, 'are you back just for this?'

'What do you mean?'

'No one sees you for years. You never write, then, one day, the day I bury my husband you appear,' her eyes burned with a beautiful blue ferocity, 'What does it mean?'

'I don't know Marie. I am very sorry I missed Jean.'

'We are all sorry,' she said, 'Did you have something to do with it?'

'What? No! I arrived yesterday. I should have been here a month ago at Christmas. I wish I had been. I would have,' I stopped, there was a flood burning in my eyes, ready to burst the dam of my resolve. I took a deep breath. 'We need to talk.'

'We do. I missed you, we all missed you.' Marie re-joined her family. Behind her came Reynard who put his arms around me. The dam broke and I let go the flood.

Behind Reynard was Dufy.

'Still a charmer with the ladies then Bassé,' Dufy said when I had calmed down.

'I am crying because Jean was such a good card player and now all I have to look forward to is beating you two dullards.' I said.

24

'We'd make you play naked at a glass table so you couldn't hide your spares,' said Dufy.

'I will ignore the slander,' I said, 'but I would still beat you every time.' I turned to Reynard, 'When was the last time either of you saw Jean?'

'Epiphany,' said Reynard, 'we'd see each other most days, living on the same street all these years.'

'And we had a game on Epiphany night,' said Dufy, 'we had fun.'

'How was he?'

'You know how he was,' said Dufy, 'sometimes up, other times down. That night he was up.'

'Any ideas?' I took shelter behind my professional gendarme's curiosity.

'He'd been playing again, out of our circle,' said Reynard, 'some southerners. He said he'd been showing them how it's done.'

'Trouble?'

'Not that he would say. I think he was quite sporting about it. Not like the old days.' Reynard shrugged.

'Not like me eh?'

'I didn't say that Stefan.'

'I know Jean-Luc. What about you Dufy?'

'Like Reynard says, nothing different,' he scratched his head, 'he liked a sure thing, like you, but always liked to chase as big a score as he could.'

I thought for a moment. 'I would have put a month's salary on Mortain swimming from here to Caen once upon a time.'

'Me too,' said Dufy, 'but not so much these days, not with the amount he still drank.'

'If you hear anything on the building site Dufy, let me know, yes?'

'Of course,' said Dufy, 'I'll keep an ear out if you think I need to.'

'I don't know,' I said, 'it could be something, it could just be my grief, but if you hear any more about these Southerners let me know.'

25

'I seem to remember one had an Italian-sounding name. Maybe he was Corsican or up from Sicily?' said Reynard, 'Something 'relli.'

'Thanks,' I said.

We shook hands and I walked past them, deeper into the cemetery. I had a visit to make.

I crossed the hallowed ground until I reached the family plot. There was my mother, Elena, a trapeze artist, and glamorous assistant on the Parisian stage, who always won applause for her grace and wit. Next to her was Grandpa, at rest, at last. I stood for a minute, not praying. I am a magician's son, so I find it hard to believe in the invisible.

When I lifted my gaze, I saw a man striding purposefully in my direction. He was familiar, but I could not quite place him. A schoolmaster perhaps? Come to pay respects to a pupil? Unlikely if he remembered me. He stopped just five metres away.

'You have balls at least Bassé,' he certainly had the pitch for a teacher, 'like your poor dead mother.'

'Excuse me?' I said.

'I am your former neighbour, Pierre de Moerlein,' he said, 'your mother was a decent woman, but your father was not a man of good standing.'

'You are entitled to your opinion sir,' I said.

'And you sir, are you a trickster and a charlatan too?'

'I am a police inspector sir, and I would respectfully remind you that I am paying a visit, after many years away, to my remaining relatives in Bayeux.'

'A policeman?' He raised his eyebrows, 'Poacher turned gamekeeper.'

'I don't think so sir,' I said, 'can I ask what you are doing here? It wasn't to meet me was it?'

'No,'

'Were you here for the funeral?'

'No young man,' he sighed, and his shoulders sagged, 'When you get to my age Inspector Bassé, you will find that the greater part of your friends and relatives all share this same address.'

Chapter Three.

My father had been a renowned illusionist, a magician of fame in Paris, accompanied by my mother, Elena Tarantelli, a trapeze artist. My father was The Great Romanovsko, born of a long line of travelling showmen. Grandpa, the Amazing Andromedus, lived out his last days with us in Bayeux, where he taught me sleight of hand, card tricks, and how to read a deck of cards and win at piquet, belote and many other games the uninitiated thought was all luck.

The Great Romanovsko became famous in Paris and made a small fortune on his reputation for ingenuity. The trick he was best known for was making his assistant, my mother, appear glittering and dry from inside what the audience knew to be a full barrel of wine. There was a tap, in the proper place, and wine flowed from it when it was open. The magician would take a draft during a balancing illusion earlier in the show which established the fact. There were critics, naturally, but the prestige of such a trick was one that the hardened audiences of France's capital city met with applause time after time.

The magician's trade was one of engineering and ingenuity. Sorcery was banned and practitioners in France were either executed or exiled during the Revolution. Practical illusions, such as my father's, celebrated the human realm and could be learned safely.

This family business had been running for generations. Grandpa had stories stretching back to the time of Peter the Great, Tsar of Russia, and talked of wild forest shamans and Egyptian Queens, how he outsmarted werewolves and caught fish that set him riddles. I never tired of his stories, told as they were with a clear-eyed view of what could happen to a person who made just one bad decision. He had seen all the capital cities of Europe and travelled as far East as the Arabian deserts, where he had met my grandmother. She had been a Muslim Princess, the youngest of five children in a royal household said to have been centuries old. He would swear I was descended from the famed Arabian Knight Saladin. He told me stories of how this great man had pushed the Crusaders out of Jerusalem and united the desert lands from the Gulf of Arabia to the Nile.

Grandpa had put on a show for a Sultan, who had been so impressed he demanded the Amazing Andromedus remain in the palace for his amusement. In reality, he had been made prisoner and could not come and go as he pleased. He remained within the walls of the palace for nearly two years, devising new illusions and entertainments for his captor. The workshop he had been given became the blueprint for all future spaces, and it was where he developed his signature Green Dragon firework recipe, one that he passed on to me before he died. I don't think I will ever part with that parchment, let alone sell it on, or even attempt to mix the formula.

Eventually, with the help of the Sultan's daughter, the lovers escaped under cover of a vanishing trick that filled the building with colourful smoke, while fireworks exploded in the night sky. He had worked hard and set off eleven Green Dragons. They circled the sky, blowing fiery sparks against the stars. By the time the Sultan had realised his magician and daughter were missing they were many leagues away, far from his reach. Grandpa and the Princess fled North to the Crimea where they were married in a little chapel in a village on the shore of the Black Sea, but in truth, they never stopped running.

Grandpa found work with a travelling show and together he and Grandma lived on the road for the rest of their lives, raising my father in the back of an oxcart. I believe it was the precarity of this situation that moved my father to make a more secure foundation for my childhood.

All magic, my father was fond of saying, was nine-tenths preparation for that one moment of perfect illusion. As a small boy, I would wait and watch in the wings. I particularly liked the animal acts, but there were fewer in the theatre. In the travelling shows there had been more. I remembered the elephants best, with their royal demeanour and reassuring mass.

There had been a real dragon in the travelling show too, for a short time, attracted by the bright lights and attention. She became part of the fire-eater's act. Grandpa said Grandma would read poetry to her. He made me learn sonnets by heart. 'It's the best way to calm a dragon down,' he said, 'recite a bit of poetry and they won't burn your wagon. Whatever you do, don't run away. They'll respect you for it.'

There's still a dragon at the Palace of Versailles, and in most of the European royal palaces, after all, they seem to enjoy the finer things in life. A dragon in the wild, or at a travelling show is rarer these days.

While my family was most certainly from the circus tradition, with its creatures and people with peculiar talents, my father maintained that we were not of it. Real magic and its proper craft and presentation was a higher art. Any fool could paint his face and throw a bucket of water about and call it an act.

His ambition stretched right across the Atlantic, to New York, but he could not make it across the English Channel. He was no sailor and was sick from Calais to Dover and back again. Eventually, other, younger practitioners of the art stole his limelight with newer tricks using the latest inventions and modern methods. He and my mother retired from the stage, and we came to Bayeux where I was to receive a proper education and lead a sensible, normal life.

*

It was in school that I met Jean Mortain, and in the back row where I tormented him with my card tricks.

'What are you doing, Bassé?' He would ask, even though it was obvious. I was shuffling a pack of cards, carefully, silently, making only the most necessary of movements to avoid detection. The teacher, Monsieur Lamotte, had a monotone drone that seemed designed to send all of us unruly children to sleep. Cards were how I resisted. They were not allowed in school, but caps and coats were perfect for hiding contraband.

I fanned the pack wide in my left hand below the desk.

'Pick one,' I said.

'No.' said Jean, 'I will not.'

'Do it. What are you afraid of?'

'What if?'

'Just shut up and take one before Lamotte hears you.'

Jean picked a card, trying hard to keep his shoulders rigid. Monsieur Lamotte had eyes in his ears and, we suspected, secret mirrors so he could spot mischief makers around every corner.

'Look at it but don't let me see it.' I said.

Jean was good at following instructions.

'Now put it back,' I said.

I shuffled again as we began chanting a times table. The cards vanished into the sleeve of my shirt as we continued the ritual mathematics.

When at last the bell sounded for the midday break we boys could not wait to get back out into the fresh air. The sky seemed higher than normal up there above our heads. God was not there. He was still cooped up in the cathedral while the guilty confessed their misdeeds. God was not allowed in the low-ceilinged chambers of the school. The only maths in the Bible was there to help build an ark. Thin wisps of pale white cloud floated on high like Monsieur Lamotte's hair on a windy day.

'What about my card?' said Jean at last.

'What card?' I teased him.

'The one I picked during maths? I thought you might have wanted to finish the trick by the time Monsieur Lamotte finished. You had plenty of chances.'

'Now why would I do that?' I said.

'For the pay-off. The prestige!' said Jean.

'No Mortain,' I said, 'I couldn't have you shout during our time's tables, now could I? Just imagine what Lamotte would have done?'

'Why would I shout? It's just one of your card tricks,' said Jean.

'I don't know Mortain, but we are not allowed to eat in the classrooms either.' I said.

'What are you talking about Bassé?'

'Here,' I offered my friend a croissant, which he took. Boys never turn down food, and Jean took a big bite.

'You gave up on your card trick then?' he said, mouth full.

'I didn't say that.' I said.

'Do you want to know what card I picked?' he said.

'I know which card you picked,' I said.

'Alright then, what was it?'

I ripped my croissant open and thrust almost an entire half into my mouth. Jean Mortain was as suggestible as he was obedient. It was a quality I liked him for. He pulled open the rest of his croissant and revealed the three of clubs right in the middle of the soft white pastry. He dropped it as if it were on fire.

'Sapristi,' he cried, 'mother of God.'

'You see,' I said, 'I knew you would shout.'

The card was stuck firmly in the croissant as if it had been baked in. It landed softly on the cobbles, card face up.

'You are in league with the Devil Bassé,' said Jean, then he turned and ran.

I could not retrieve my card for at least five minutes, I was so debilitated by my laughter.

Later, I would teach Jean more useful card tricks, and together we became almost unbeatable at the card table. He tended toward riskier behaviours than I did. A sure thing was always my favoured route. I preferred to play safe and look to the longer game, but with Jean sometimes we would win bigger than I expected. Once the stubborn Jean Mortain had decided a particular prize was his it was impossible to persuade him otherwise. Another trait that I particularly admired. Most of the time.

*

'She is so pretty.'

'Who? The brunette?' I said.

'Her, over there, the blonde.' He said.

'Well observed Mortain.'

31

'You sound like Monsieur Lamotte,' he said, 'I don't think you will ever kiss a girl Bassé.'

It was harvest time and the city was bedecked with flags and ribbons and for once the sun was out and we could stuff our caps into our belts. It was also the time of year that the travelling show came to town. The circus and fairground were set up on the waste ground out on the Eastern edge of the city, on the road that led across the old bridge. We would head out that way after school to take it all in.

Before the first show, there was always a parade, with an elephant, clowns, and a fire eater, sometimes a strange creature from beyond the mountains, but I hadn't seen a dragon in years. Father never forbade me to go, though he remained behind shuttered windows all the while the circus was in town.

Mortain and I were lanky fifteen-year-olds, ready for all the flavours of the adult world, but unsure as to how we might get a first taste. Jean was in love with Marie, the blonde, as was I. 'We should go and say hello,' I said, 'do you like her dark-haired friend?'

'She's pretty too, and tall, like you Bassé,' he said, 'but I saw the blonde first.'

'As you say,' I said, sensing trouble ahead, 'let fate take us where it may.'

We crossed the road toward the two girls. I knew they had already seen us talking about them. I'd seen them both before too. They lived on the outside of town, closer to the porcelain factories, and went to a neighbouring school. I had had my eye on Marie for a couple of months already and even managed a brief greeting after mass one Sunday. Mortain might well believe this to be a chance meeting, but nothing was further from the truth.

My father always maintained that the best surprises were planned well in advance so that nothing could go wrong. The worst that could happen was an unexpected event. He taught me to plan for those too. I had hoped that the lovely brunette Amandine would be enough to turn Mortain's head, trusting as I did in his lack of ambition. There was still time. We made our approach in short order, cramming our caps back on our heads in time to tip them to the ladies.

'Good evening mademoiselles,' I said, 'may we accompany you to the entertainments?'

The two girls giggled at us but did not look away.

'He means,' said Jean, 'would you like to come with us to the show?'

He offered his arm to Marie, but she did not notice. She was still holding my eye.

'You must be Marie,' I said, 'and your friend must be Amandine?'

'How?' said Marie as she took my arm.

'He's the son of a magician,' said Jean, which drew gasps from both girls. Jean offered Amandine his arm and she took it. Good man, I thought.

'My father engaged your father in some business or other, and they fell to discussing schools and prospects,' I said, 'and so I hear that you are a prize-winning scholar?'

'You should be a detective,' said Marie, 'but I am afraid I will have to win many more prizes if I am to escape the farm.'

'I am certain you will escape,' I said, 'and your intuition is impressive Marie, as I will be a cadet constable very soon.'

It all went well at first, but I could feel Jean's resentment like a finger stuck in my back, making me uncomfortable. I had a feeling his stubborn streak was going to win out over my need to control events.

At the circus field, Jean was straight to the point.

'See anyone you recognize among the gypsies Bassé? Any uncles or cousins? Long lost half-brothers?'

'Not so far,' I said, 'my circus days were a long time ago. I was a babe in arms really.'

'What do you remember?' asked Marie.

'Well.' I thought for a minute. What should I say? I had a selection of responses, honed over time, to deal with questions fired at me at school and elsewhere. Despite Jean's attempt to unsettle me I had, of course, anticipated the question and I had an answer that I knew Jean had not heard before. 'I remember it being summer most of the time as the travelling show followed the seasons. The elephants, they were my favourite. So gentle, so intelligent. And the lions. They always smelled of fresh meat.'

'I want to see the lions,' said Amandine. 'Where do they keep them?'

'Gott in Himmel!' It was a clown, white-faced with a single sprout of crimson hair standing up like a cock's comb over a bald pate. 'But you are the spit of him!'

'Pardon?' I said.

'What are the chances, boy?' Said the clown, 'You won't know me with this face on but my how you've grown. I was at your mother's funeral, God rest her, such a shame. So young. But Stefan, it's me, Otto.'

'What? Otto? You are a clown now?' I said, 'When did you give up throwing knives?'

'My eyes,' he said, 'I can't afford another accident.'

'What?'

'Joking, joking,' he said, 'better a clown than a dull-eyed cowboy eh?'

'Yes,' I said, 'of course.'

'Is your father coming? The Great Romanovsko.'

'No,' I said, 'I don't think he likes to be reminded.'

'Shame, shame,' said Otto. 'He was one of the greats. He truly lived up to the name. I tried to get him to come back after your mother, you know?'

'I know Otto,' I said.

'But no. He wanted to see his Stefan properly settled. Living a normal life, growing up in a civilised manner.' He clapped me on the shoulder, 'So are you?'

'What?'

'Settled? Civilised?'

'I don't know Otto, but can you get us in to see the lions?'

'As you wish sire,' Otto bowed so low I was afraid his hairpiece might fall off, 'You are circus royalty, Prince Stefan. How can I refuse your command?'

'You need better jokes, Otto,' I said.

'I believe him,' Marie squeezed my arm, 'I like to think I am going to the circus with a Prince.'

Behind me, I could feel Mortain boiling away.

Otto led us around the back of a row of stalls and we ducked behind a tarpaulin. In a moment, the world was changed, and I was immediately transported back to my early years steeped in the reek of paint and old rope, wood smoke and the spoor of very big cats. We passed through the shadows to the lion tamer's wagons. In one was a pair of males with huge manes, lying in repose, licking their paws.

'They wake up in the evening, so we feed them a little bit before the show to keep them calm,' said Otto, 'but not so much that they fall asleep.'

'They are incredible,' said Marie, 'I have never been so close to such dangerous beasts.'

'You only just met Stefan Bassé,' laughed Jean, who had forgotten his stubborn jealousy of a few minutes before.

Together we approached the caged lions. The scent was overpowering. I took Marie's hand and together we patted the golden flank of one of the males. He yawned, bored, ignoring our touch.

'Hey Stefan,' said Otto, 'if you have room up your sleeve for a little something for my act, I will get you all in ringside.'

I looked at Marie. She was mesmerised by the lions.

'What do you say, Stefan,' said Otto, 'in or wet chicken?'

'I am the grandson of the Amazing Andromedus,' I said, 'in, of course.'

I smiled to myself. Everything appeared to be working out as I had planned.

*

Otto had managed to get us front-row seats, which were highly prized, but it did mean you were more likely to get a wetting from the water thrown about by the clowns. I watched Marie as she watched the skill and daring of the trapeze artists. She was in awe of the lion tamer and held onto my arm as the beasts stalked the ring inside their cage. I tried not to yawn while the current magician pulled handkerchiefs from his sleeves and produced white doves from his hat. A giant orc entered the ring and showed his prowess at lifting heavy things and bending iron bars. He sent shudders around the audience. To me, he looked old, tired, and humiliated.

When Otto arrived in his patchwork trousers and white painted face, I sat up ready. He wore a top hat like the magician had, and he paraded around the ring in mockery of the conjurer's act. He lifted off his hat and sawdust spilt all over his shoulders. The crowd laughed. Then he came to me, hat tilted at a crazy angle on his head, and mimed falling in love with Marie. He was very good. Then he turned to me and went to shake my hand. I held up my hand and with a deft move, Otto pulled a bouquet of roses from out of my sleeve and handed it to Marie with a deep bow.

When she took the flowers, he fell over backwards and was immediately set upon by a crowd of clowns who had taken that as their cue to invade the ring. Mayhem ensued with the clowns tumbling and putting on an incredible acrobatic display that delighted us all. At the end came the buckets of water. We were lucky not to get soaked.

Chapter Four.

Paris was a beautiful but difficult place for a young policeman to progress. I was no Javert. I did not have his certainties, even though I felt his ambition was mine. The criminal classes in the city would use the flag when it pleased them and stood for anything that could make them money. I lost the battle as soon as I joined the commissariat in my arrondissement, and immediately I began looking for a way out. In those days, volunteering overseas looked like the best option. After two years I was sent to Cayenne, the capital of French Guyana in South America, and home to the notorious Devil's Island penitentiary.

The posting was hard. All of France's least wanted, beggars, thieves, shapeshifters and worse were sent across the Atlantic to take their chances. After six months or more in jail most remained in Cayenne or one of the squalid townships along the coast. Before long they were either back in jail or dead. It was not a happy place.

For the most part, I was there for crowd control, keeping order on feast days and any other day when a riot might break out. Most of all I was there for promotion, which came quicker in the outposts of the empire, where the law was sometimes a less rigorous institution than the one I recognized from my training. We were encouraged to be creative, but some went far beyond what I would recognize as legal means. Early on I spoke out, but it only brought me trouble.

In Cayenne, it seemed I had much more in common with Javert than my colleagues liked. I was relentless in the pursuit of one fellow in particular, Michel St-Pol. He was a thief and a murderer who traded in gold, stole gold, and used it to bribe the gendarmeries in seven cantons. Rumour had it he fed his werewolves on human flesh.

In truth, everyone in the city was here to make money and few cared where it came from. A captain in the gendarmerie hoped to accumulate enough to buy the mayor's office on his return to France, settle old scores, and play the King, if he lived long enough. St-Pol was one of those who aimed to help these tawdry ambitions.

My problem with this bandit was quite simply the sheer scale of his disregard for life, whether human or otherwise. It almost made me feel sorry for the wolf-men he kept like dogs and the other creatures that he used for his amusement. He would shoot a man for a single gold ring, kill another for a nugget not worth a sou. But all the time he enriched my comrades in arms, they remained his protectors.

'Just take your cut and keep quiet Bassé,' was my Captain's refrain, 'you'll be Mayor of Bayeux when you're forty.'

'But Captain Verrier I don't want to be Mayor of anywhere.'

'Not now you don't.'

'I don't even want to go back to Bayeux.' I insisted.

'Then found a new city in Canada, somewhere like Quebec where there are no savages left anymore and only Frenchmen to be Mayor of.'

'I just want to be a policeman,' I said, 'I want to serve the law. I don't want to take the money of criminals and serve them instead.'

'Don't get all high and mighty with me young man,' he said, 'or you will find yourself in difficulties with the rest of the men. It's not a good idea to make yourself unpopular around here.'

'I'll just do my duty sir.' I said.

'Good,' said Verrier, 'Just mind how you go about it.'

I soon learned who I could bring in and who I had to let go by. Drunks and beggars became my stock in trade for those first years. It was always the same names and faces, for a while they might sober up, move away, or simply drop dead, but others would take their place. Many of them were newly released from the island penitentiary, but without any means or hope of a return to France, they fell into lawlessness.

Most days I felt like a street cleaner. I had my patch and I swept it every day. I found a routine punctuated by stops at coffee houses at one end and slums at the other. The coffee was usually peerless, strong, and thick as molasses.

People would talk in the coffee houses. I would sit and listen to tales of gold prospecting in the jungles, of encounters with the native people who lived on the rivers and stories of how the local police had done them wrong. There was a tale of how a band of wolf-folk had tried to make a home in the jungle, hunting the peculiar skinny mountain deer, and the giant water rats. How they visited Cayenne and stole away the drunks from the side of the road in the middle of the night. I took it all with a pinch of salt. People loved stories, and there was no shortage of roadside drunks.

'Hey Bassé,' no one called me constable in this coffee house.

'Yes, Didier?' I said.

Didier was the proprietor of this establishment, a shack on a street corner that never seemed to close. The man himself was as weathered as the boards that clad the place, worn to a coffee-coloured sheen by constant traffic.

'You know what happened in here last night?' he said.

'Of course not. I was asleep, unlike some.'

'That card cheat Boucher was in here taking everyone for their gold,' Didier was as upset as I had ever seen him.

'If it means that much perhaps you should ban him?' I said, 'It's your place. You don't have to let him in.'

'For my shame I do,' he hung his head, 'I have no choice.'

'What do you mean?'

'He has a share in my business.'

'What?' I was nonplussed, 'You and Boucher? Business partners?'

He nodded.

'I find that hard to believe.'

'It's true,'

'Is it protection? Do you have to pay him?'

'Half the profit is his, not that it's very much.'

'What?'

'He owns half my place,'

'How long?'

'A year next month.'

'Boucher bought a half share, why? Who did you owe money to Didier?' I could see the answer written on his face.

'I wasn't in any kind of trouble until I sat down at the card table with him.'

39

'I see.'

'He had been losing to his friends and getting drunk.'

'And you saw a chance for some easy money.' It was not a question.

'I won at first, a little bit. Then I lost a little bit.' Didier stared at the floor.

'Then my friend, he let you win a little more, but not too much.' I sipped at my coffee, unable to shift the frown that had come to rest on my brow at this news.

'No,' Didier shook his head, 'I won a lot. Almost enough to get me back to France, if not to America.'

'Then what happened?'

'I put it all on the table, along with the café,' said Didier, 'I felt invincible.'

'All or nothing?'

Didier nodded. 'But Boucher was sporting and would only let me bet half the shop.'

'And then you lost,' I said, 'and still you lose every day.'

'He wouldn't let me play again. Said I had nothing left worth putting up as a stake.'

'What is half your café worth?'

'I don't know,' Didier shrugged, 'less now.'

I knew of Boucher. He was an associate of St-Pol who collected people rather than killing them. I was not sure which was worse. His method was to hire or buy people into his network. Before long they would find themselves in debt to him for food or lodging, or advances made on already poor wages.

The weak and the vulnerable would be taken on and used up, building a slum Boucher called Neuilly, on an old plantation. He fancied himself as mayor of a new town in this new world. A place with no church, no school, and no doctor. All it had was a bank and a cemetery.

I already had a dossier on St-Pol and had recently started another on Boucher. I planned to gather all the evidence I could and then present it to the prefect's office.

But this expansion into my patch, into my local coffee house, felt personal.

'When does he come in here, Didier?'

'He comes in once every two weeks for his money and every other night for dinner. He will be in tomorrow night at about nine and play cards with friends or associates he has found somewhere. He won't be bringing them here to impress.'

'Who does he play?'

'Any fool like me who thinks he knows cards.'

'What are you making tomorrow,' I asked, 'ratatouille?'

'Of course,' he said, 'just like every night for the last ten years.'

'Then I will be in tomorrow night at eight-thirty.'

'What for?'

'Ratatouille Didier,' I said, 'ratatouille.'

'He's not going to want to play cards with a gendarme.'

'I've got a pot of money just like every other policeman in this town.'

'You're not on the take like the rest of them though.'

'True enough Didier. There are better ways to make a little extra money here and there and our friend Boucher won't know what I do for a living if I leave my uniform at the barracks.'

'I don't know Bassé, he's a cunning one.'

'Well,' I said, 'we will have to see what happens then.'

I have always had an unshakeable confidence in my ability to read a deck of cards, the same way a chef can walk into a kitchen and turn raw milk, eggs, and flour into any number of delights. Grandpa was a good, if somewhat impatient teacher, but I was a quick learner and an eager student.

It was not long before I was devising my own card tricks, memorising decks of cards, and using sleight of hand and misdirection to vanish and reappear Kings, Queens, Jacks, and Aces. I was certain I would be a match for Boucher.

That evening I dressed up in my one fancy shirt and my best pair of trousers. I wanted to make a decent impression but not overdo it. I broke open my safe box in the bottom of my trunk and retrieved as much coin as I could carry. It was what I'd won from my comrades in small-stakes card games. It was the legitimate way of relieving them of their bribes.

At Didier's place, the air was full of the aromas of ratatouille and pork ribs. I ordered a plateful and settled down to enjoy

41

some fine workmen's food before I got to business. It is hard to play a good game on an empty stomach.

I was halfway through when Boucher arrived with two other men. Didier was on hand to point him out but there was no need. Boucher looked just like his traditional jolly, fat namesake. One of his companions looked like he was there to break noses to order, the other was fresh off the boat and already sweating in the tropical night air.

Didier fussed about, buzzing like a mayfly all over the place. I waited until he had settled Boucher then called him over.

'Waiter,' I shouted, 'over here,' grabbing Boucher's attention at the same time. I was given a cursory once-over.

'Yes sir?' said Didier.

I lowered my voice. 'Get me some water in a gin bottle my friend.'

'Right away sir,' he said, clearing my plate. I passed him a gold coin but managed to drop it, so it rolled over in Boucher's direction.

'Sorry,' I shrugged and let Didier run after the coin under Boucher's table. I raised my glass in a toast to Boucher, who acknowledged me with a smirk. His nose-breaking associate put his foot over the coin and so Didier abandoned it.

I sat and drank my false gin for a half hour while Boucher ate with his two companions. Once they had finished and the table had been cleared away, he produced a pack of cards and began to shuffle. I jumped up straight away and in two strides I was face to face with the man.

'Apologies for throwing my coin around earlier. I had a good day at another table in town.'

'Good for you,' he grunted. Nose-breaker eyed me.

'I see you play?' I said.

'I don't play,' said Boucher, 'children play. My cards are for art.'

'Art?' I put on a stupefied expression and took a swig from my gin bottle.

'I like to make an exhibition of the people I beat.'

'Oh, very good,' I said, holding on to the edge of the table, 'and do you beat many?'

'Everyone,' he said, 'every time.'

'Well, that would be worth seeing.'

'I have a rendezvous this evening with these two fine cardsmen, monsieur Villeneuve,' he indicated the thug, 'and monsieur Montmorency.'

I exchanged nodded greetings with the two men. Montmorency made a strange bloodless half-smile.

'May I be permitted to join this threesome?' I asked, lowering my bag of gold onto the table. 'I have not brought too much out with me tonight, but I am hopeful it will suffice for I am always pleased to see a master of the craft at work.'

'You may be disappointed when you go home without your bag of gold,' said Boucher.

'I have another,' I shrugged, 'but, I am feeling lucky tonight.'

'I am Monsieur Boucher,' he said, 'and you?'

'Reynard,' I said. We shook hands at last, and I sat.

Boucher dealt and, following his boast, he beat us all in what was quite a breathtaking display of card playing. I was quite awestruck. He was a master, and I was in distinct danger of losing everything. He won the second game and the third. I saw Montmorency begin to wilt but then buck up as he won the fourth by a whisker. I watched Villeneuve closely throughout. He was Boucher's man, taking signals and playing a second hand for his boss. I had a feeling I was in line to make a small win on the next hand. It was a solid time-served system. Make them lose just enough to worry them, then let them win a little back. Repeat the process then wind the play up to an all-stakes final act and bring the hammer down taking everything left on the table.

I drank from my gin bottle steadily, but not so much that I should be seen as a drunk, but just enough to reassure Boucher I was no real threat, so by the time I had my first win, courtesy of the host, I had memorised most of the pack and could read it as if it were dealt face up.

I broke Boucher's game in the next hand, winning when I was not meant to. I had watched the subtle exchanges between him and Villeneuve all night and began to be able to decode their silent talk as well.

Before he got cold feet, I let him beat me in the next hand. As he raked in his winnings, he let out a yawn, code for calling time.

'One more game,' I said, 'let us finish with a proper bet.'

'A what?' said Boucher.

'Well, we have been spoiled with your artistry tonight sir,' I said, 'but I am sure there are still sights to be seen.'

'Maybe Reynard, but I am not as young as you, and I have had a long day.'

'But your age should not mean you cannot beat me again.' I gave him a lop-sided smile.

'I will beat you as many times as I like.' Boucher covered his mouth with the back of his hand.

'Here,' I put my bag of gold in the middle of the table, 'I have so much left and I am leaving tomorrow.'

'Where are you going?' Suddenly Boucher seemed to revive.

'A place where there are no card players of your calibre, I assure you.'

'America then?' said Boucher, 'You poor fellow. I will leave you with a final game you will not forget young man. Montmorency? You in?'

Montmorency nodded, then shook his head. 'I will watch and learn sir,' he said.

Boucher did not need to ask Villeneuve. It was clear he would be supporting his boss in this final show.

I pushed the stakes as high as I dared, but Boucher met them and raised them again. I could read his hand and Villeneuve's from across the table, which meant he could read mine too. If I kept my cards closed it made it harder for him, so I was quick to pick up. The sleight of hand I had learned from Grandpa helped. Time crept past and the stakes rose to a point where I turned my money bag inside out.

Boucher's face was immobile, carved from a yellowish stone, but his eyes raged. I had cards in my hand that should not have been there. They were cards from his pack, but he had no part in putting them in play. I watched as he spun cards from the bottom of the pack, but we both knew they would not be enough. There was so much at stake for me on the table. It would take me six months of steady card playing in the barracks to make it back.

I was not worried. My full house was unbeatable.

'A fine exhibition sir,' I said, shovelling the coin back into my bag. I had more than doubled my money. 'I may return one day and beat you again.'

'I don't think so.' Said Boucher. He stood up and turned his back on me. 'You won't find me in here again.'

'Why ever not sir?'

'Because tonight I will burn it down.'

'What?'

'It has brought me bad luck, so now it has to go,' growled Boucher.

'But monsieur,' I began.

'Quit, boy, while you are ahead,' said Boucher, 'my patience has limits if my purse has not.'

I shrugged, 'Of course,' what else was there to say? When he left, taking Villeneuve and Montmorency with him, Didier came across and rested a hand on my shoulder.

'You did what you could mon ami,' he said.

'I schooled him at his own crooked game,' I said, 'but I fear I have made things much worse for you now.'

'With this place gone I will not stay,' Didier shrugged, 'it's for the best.'

'Where will you go?'

'Who knows Stefan?'

'Here,' I handed him my money bag, 'this belongs to you.'

'No, my friend, I cannot take it.'

'I insist Didier. Before this evening at least you owned half of something. Now I have lost even that for you.'

He took the bag from me and looked inside.

'With this perhaps I will be able to go home.'

'Where's that Didier?'

'Provence, my friend. Draguignan, in the Mediterranean foothills of the Alps.' Didier smiled, 'You will visit me there one day.'

'That I will, Didier,' I said.

45

The next morning, I walked the lanes back to Didier's shack and discovered that, true to his promise, Boucher had razed the place to the ground. All that remained were a few smoking stumps of wood and the stink of burnt fat. We found Didier a week later in the harbour. His throat had been cut.

Chapter Five.

At the commissariat Sergeant Royer was quick with the coffee. I took my time opening up the shutters in my office. The sills were still frosted with ice and the coffee stung my nose in the sharp air. A pigeon landed on the windowsill. It made me think of the parrots in South America. I did not miss Guyana, not yet, and I certainly did not miss being far from Marie.

I shuddered. I felt awkward meeting the old crowd on such a strange occasion, appearing like a spectre at the feast, unannounced. I was grateful for their warm welcome but was angry at the timing of my return and upset by the strange old man.

I do not know what I was expecting. The disappearance of my father had ensured that my personal Bayeux would be different. I am not so sure I would have taken the posting had he still been here. His absence was a change I could live with, for now. But for all my travels and time spent abroad, not sending many, and receiving fewer letters, I expected most other things to have remained reasonably unchanged. Dufy was always going to follow his uncles onto the building site and Reynard moved into his father's workshop as sure as night follows day. There was an order, almost a predestination to the world I left behind, running on a set of tracks that led into the future and reached back as far as anyone could remember.

When I signed the papers accepting the responsibilities of the Bayeux Commissariat, I thought friendships would be picked up simply where they left off over a kitchen table. Seeing Marie again was always bound to be complicated, but I had relied on the passage of time to have cooled the passions. I had hoped that she and Jean were happy.

I did not know what to think now. Death was a daily truism in the shanties of Cayenne. I thought I had become inured, immune to the fact that life can end brutally, sometimes quietly, and often without comment. I thought of monsieur de Moerlein and decided at once that I should always look to make acquaintances in new places in case I too should be left a lonely visitor in the future.

The dossier on Jean Mortain lay on my desk exactly where I had left it. I nudged it to one side and tried not to look directly at it. I turned my chair sideways and sipped my coffee. Also, on the table, on a small plate was a pain-au-chocolat. I blessed Royer and his family. He had a brother who was an exceptional baker. I pulled at the pastry and mopped up the last of the coffee.

Revived, I turned back to the dossier, opened the file, and ran my finger down the page until I came to a name, 'Madame Osment?' I called down to Royer, 'Where can I find this woman?'

Royer coughed into his hand, 'She may be found in the row of hovels next to the river. She runs a rough-house bar on the Rue Tire-Vit. She does not give us any trouble. Last house before the bridge.'

'Tire-Vit?' I said, 'It doesn't have a name yet does it?'

'No, but you know where it is?'

'I do, thank you, Sergeant,' I said, 'I will be discreet. What do you know of her opening hours?'

'I wouldn't know sir, but it is busy along there early in the evening when the factories turn out. It doesn't tend to go late as the road is so poor.'

'Thank you, Sergeant. Is there a horse for my use?'

'Yes sir, Magpie sir. I will see to it now.'

'Very good Royer.'

I finished my coffee quickly and went to meet my new horse in the rear yard. She had already been saddled and made ready for me. I approached and she snorted out a cloud of breath, nodding gently. There were white flashes on her head and along her nose, which I guessed had gifted her name. I took her reins, stroked her between the eyes and patted her neck. She regarded me with a dark eye and let out a quiet snort.

'I think we might be friends,' I told her, 'And you look tough enough to take on the enemy.'

I hoisted myself up into the saddle and Magpie settled beneath me.

'Who had this mare before I did, Sergeant?'

'She has only been here a week,' said Royer, 'So someone somewhere must think highly of you.'

'Mere chance, Royer,' I said, 'not that I'm ungrateful.'

I patted Magpie's neck once more and set her off at a walk out of the yard.

Before long, I was crossing the city to one of its least impressive areas, far from the long shadows of the famous cathedral. The Rue Tire-Vit was not an official name even though so many towns of this size had similar streets. The mayor would eventually decree a new nameplate to obscure a tradition I too would rather see the end of.

The bridge at this crossing of the Aure was quite ancient and in absolute need of replacement. It was often blocked with flotsam after a storm. There were no trolls left to keep the river clear these days, at least, not in modern, post-revolutionary France. I imagine there are some left across the other side of the Black Sea and in the frozen wastes of Canada, where certain things are better left beyond the reach of progress and modernisation. Grandpa was sure things had been better before people went and changed everything, but isn't that what every grandpa thinks? I'm sure I'll be the same one day.

The report on Mortain stated that it was here right by the old bridge, that the body of my friend had been discovered. Madame Osment had wasted no time in reporting the find to the sergeant at the commissariat. A corpse at the front door was no good for business.

I was certain Mortain was a customer. His only mistress lived at the bottom of a bottle.

I knocked lightly on the door, and it sprang open as if I had been expected. I doffed my hat and enquired after the mistress of the house.

'Do come in sir,' the girl was as tall and dark as the women I met in Guyana. Her voice had a familiar lilt. I ducked inside.

The doors were set in this way to slow entry and deter a hurried exit. I was shown to a rug-covered chaise.

'Would sir like an aperitif?' asked the girl.

'I am here on business mademoiselle,' I said, 'and I would like to speak with madame Osment as a matter of urgency.'

'I am afraid she is sleeping at the moment. The madame had a long night, but,' she cocked her head to the doorway at the bar at the back of the room, 'I can assure you sir that I am very proficient in serving beer, cider, or perhaps a stronger aperitif, even at this early hour.'

'I wish I could say that I am pleased to hear it,' I said, 'however I am not here for that. I am a policeman investigating a murder.'

At this, the girl's disposition changed.

'Yes sir,' she said, and, lifting her skirts, she disappeared through a doorway at the back of the room. I followed, having thrown the bolt on the front door. I cursed myself for rushing out alone and not putting officers on all sides of the building.

She skipped upstairs and when she disappeared onto the landing at the top, I followed her as quietly as I could. I peered around the corner on the landing into a dim hallway. The air reeked of animal sweat and cheap perfume. The girl was standing in the doorway of a room just a few paces away. Satisfied she was not trying for an escape I retreated to the bottom of the stairs and cleared my throat.

'Madame is coming,' called the girl.

I remained at the bottom of the stairs waiting for the sound of footsteps. When I saw the top of the staircase darken, I retreated to the chaise. In Paris, this sort of establishment was far more sophisticated with multiple exits and at least two staircases. This was much meaner. With only the one main door it was not far above a stable.

'Good morning sir,' Madame Osment arrived like an apparition, doused with powder, and hung about with lace. It had been a day for ghosts. 'I am at the service of the gendarmerie at all times.'

I stood for her and made a small polite bow. I waved her to the chaise. She sat.

'Thank you, madame,' I remained standing, 'I am Inspector Bassé. Please forgive my insistence on seeing you so suddenly but I fear time is running out for me with this particular investigation.'

'Is it to do with the poor man I found?'

'Madame, were you acquainted?'

'So sad, poor man,' she said, 'I am certain I didn't know him although his face did seem familiar at the time.'

'What happened? How did you discover the man?'

'I was on my way out early as I had to pay some bills and get provisions. The night had been busy, my hotel was full, and I wanted to make sure there was enough in the larder. They get hungry playing cards and drinking.'

'Yes,' I said. I thought the word hotel was an ambitious view of the establishment, but I let it go.

'Well, there I was, all wrapped up because of the cold. It was bitter out and it was foggy too. I always have trouble with my chest if I go out unprotected into the damp air,' she shuddered, 'and there he was in the reeds right by the bank. It was a terrible shock.'

'I am certain that it was madame,' I said.

'I mean, I have seen a thing or two in my short time here on God's earth, but not many dead men, poor thing.' She dabbed at her eyes with a corner of a lace handkerchief.

'What happened next madame?'

'Well, my first thought was to see if he was alright. I know it sounds silly now when I say it, I mean the river had frozen around him, but I thought he must be cold. I worried he would catch his death, it not being clear from where I was standing, I suppose. I was hoping he wasn't dead.'

I nodded. 'Then what?'

'Then I stepped out carefully onto the ice and called out to him. Then I poked him with the toe of my boot, and that's when I caught the smell of him.'

Madame Osment dabbed again at her eyes with the lace handkerchief, either in grief or in remembrance of the smell. I could not say.

'Was there anyone else on the bankside with you or on the bridge madame?'

'No Inspector. I was quite alone. But when I returned with the sergeant and his men there was a little crowd of onlookers. Your man saw them off to a distance then broke the poor gentleman out of the ice.'

'Was there anyone in the crowd you recognized or were surprised to see?'

'A couple of my staff had come to look, my cook and kitchen boy and I thought I saw the young stable lad from the Hotel du Theatre. He's foreign, I think, and he has a thing for my barmaid, who you just met, but he is so young and so shy he has hardly been through our door.'

'Thank you, madame,' I said, 'I am minded to invite all your staff into the commissariat for statements, just in case they saw something unusual.'

'I don't think they would like that.' Madame Osment shuddered and blew her nose into her lace handkerchief.

'It is not such a quiet street, and I must believe someone must have heard or seen something,' I took out my pocketbook and pencil, 'can we start with names and dates of birth?'

The barkeeper watched as I drew up two columns on a page and slowly wrote her name at the top of the first.

'That might take a terribly long time, Inspector, and I am certain none of them saw anything or they would have told me.'

I remained silent and instead began to number the lines on the page.

'I did know him,' she said, 'His name was Jean, but he wasn't a customer as much as a host to other customers. He would bring men here and play them at cards in the back room and take their money while they were distracted by drink. We took their money too. They were never any trouble. My cook sees to that sort of thing, and they did no more than take up space in the bedrooms with their snoring.'

'Better,' I said, 'When was the last time Jean was here?'

'Almost a month. It was the full moon, and it's coming up again in a few days. His friends, or whatever they were, none of them have been back.'

'Are you certain of the date madame?'

'Quite certain.' She made a show of blowing her nose once more, 'Jean would go for weeks without knocking on our door, then there would be a few months when he would come every week.'

'What did Jean do when these other men went upstairs?'

'He would leave,' she said, 'he had work somewhere in the city to do. Something ordinary. Not my words, but that was all he would say.'

'Was it always the same men or were they different every time madame?'

'I think they were journeymen for the most part. Here for a short time on the new building sites or some other work.' She shrugged, 'Their money all looked the same.'

'I see,' I said, 'thank you, madame, you have been most helpful.'

'I have?'

'Indeed,' I closed my notebook, 'that will be all for now.'

Madame Osment stood up and we shook hands. She showed me out and as the door thudded closed behind me, I found myself standing on the riverbank. Ice had built up around the bridge, sticks and other flotsam crowded around its narrow arches. A patch of shattered and refrozen ice marked the spot where Jean had been found. I could still see the troll chair, built into the bank. They used to fish and keep the arches of the bridges clear of debris, but between the tanneries and the porcelain works poisoning the water, and the revolution, the trolls were long gone.

Poor Jean. Gone too, forever. Drunk and drowned? Had it come to that? Was murder so much better? Something was not right about these circumstances, but I had no evidence to back up the uneasy feeling I had in my gut.

I stepped out onto the frozen river and looked closely at the broken water where his body had been given up. I thought I could see remnants of a shirt encased in the ice. It was hard to tell.

I shuddered and turned away and thought I might follow the rotten track of the Tire-Vit upstream, past a row of hovels where other men and women waited, shivering in the damp, for the world to get better. The river had kept my friend's secret for almost a month. But it might never have confessed to hiding him at all.

The sun was still shining but it gave no warmth. The wind had picked up and the cold air bit through my coat like the winter wolf. I shuddered on the path, listening to the music of the ice as it split and broke away in the current, flowing off to Jean's bridge. What a miserable, desolate place to be discovered.

I cast around for any sign that might have been preserved since he entered the river, but the search rendered nothing of interest. Ice caught and preserved but also moved and changed.

After a little way, I turned back and returned to the bridge where I had tied Magpie. She had waited, silent and unperturbed. I took the ride back into town at a slow pace, my mind turning over and over the circumstances of Jean's death. My mood was dark when I arrived back at the commissariat. This was so far away from the homecoming I had envisaged. I was not so sentimental as to believe there would be flags and a parade, but this was worse than my darkest imaginings.

The path to my office cleared before me, even Sergeant Royer turned away and found something that demanded close attention in his ledger. A silence spread through the building around me, for which I was grateful. I sat at my desk and sunk into a low state of contemplation, my mind working over what I did and did not know. I was not certain there was even a case. Next to me on the desk, a stack of dossiers and other paperwork had appeared. It was all of the administrative process that keeps a department such as this on the straight and narrow. Some of my colleagues would forever complain that it slowed them down, held them up, or impeded their progress in the day-to-day pursuit of criminals.

I, however, knew that without it a constable might have to wait longer for new boots, or a roof repair may be delayed, causing more expense, and, of course, more paperwork. It is the oil in the gears of the machine of justice. As such I could not disregard this duty.

I took the first paper from the top of the pile. My approval was sought for the farrier's bill. It had already been checked and signed by Durand the accountant. He has been here more than thirty years now and has a solid reputation with all our suppliers. I put my name in the space allotted to it and turned to the next item.

I continued in this way until the light began to fade. It was still getting dark early, at around five in the afternoon on a cloudless day. I could feel the temperature falling as it got darker. I could have continued with the lamp light, but I was overcome with a sudden fatigue I felt seeping all the way down into my bones.

I was bound to spend another night at the Hotel de Ville. I was not yet ready to face the old house. It held too many memories for a heart to cope with at the end of a day like today. I knew Reynard and Dufy would be raising a glass in Mortain's name tonight, but I just wanted to sleep it all away. I left the commissariat without a word to anyone, but with my dark mood somewhat reduced by the comfort of routine paperwork. As before, it was as if the men could read my inner feelings. No one looked my way, and all appeared absorbed by whatever task they were bent to. Perhaps they had become used to there being no captain to guide their ship. There was no excuse for such self-indulgence on my part. I had a duty to perform and perform it I must, no matter what personal suffering I might endure.

As my mother always told me, 'The show must go on.'

And so it would. Tomorrow.

I left the building like a shadow, like the ghost of the cadet who had begun his policing career here so many years ago. So many conflicting thoughts. I knew this posting would not be easy, but for it to have begun in such an inauspicious way was difficult for me to understand. But, again, as a wise person once said to me, we weren't here because we had all the answers, we were here because we had so many questions.

But why did all the questions have to be so hard?

The thought of a hot bath at the hotel cheered me. A simple pleasure. It was so cold here in Bayeux in January. I had forgotten the Normandy winters in my constant summer state in the tropics. There were seasons, but they were marked by whether or not there were hurricanes. The Normandaise folk complained about the rain as often as they could. It was traditional, but having experienced the way it rains in Guyana I saw nothing to moan about here apart from the aching cold. I shivered. At least the blood in my veins remained warm.

Chapter Six.

Sergeant Royer was sitting in the staff canteen with his fellow old hand, Constable Henri Mouche, sipping his morning coffee and dipping croissants and coming to terms with the latest changes at the Bayeux Commissariat, out of sight of the man himself.

'Would you believe it?' said Sergeant Royer, 'I wouldn't have bet a thousand Francs on his return, but here he is. It's Bassé's ship now.

'I'm not much for travelling myself,' Royer was in an expansive mood, 'I've been to Rouen and Le Havre but don't like big, smoky cities, with more factory chimneys than church spires. You can keep Paris as far as I'm concerned. Madame Royer has talked about taking the train to the next Exposition. Go and see the new tower. She can go on her own.'

He sighed. The arrival of their youthful new boss made Royer feel his age.

'I always liked him,' said Mouche.

'What?' Royer laughed. He laughed like an old donkey who had smoked too many pipes, making the noise on the inhale, and coughing on the exhale. 'You never did, the boy showed you up at cards too many times.'

'True,' sighed Mouche, 'I always hoped they'd skin him alive in Paris.'

'I know, said Royer, 'and when I heard he was off to South America I thought - that's it, he's a goner.'

'I thought he'd be eaten by wild animals. Is he back here for very long?'

'I don't know Mouche, but it seems the man might be luckier than either of us suspected.' Royer stroked his moustache. It was getting thicker and wirier as the years passed, resembling an old yard broom. But he didn't care.

Mouche shrugged. 'He survived Paris and the jungle. Must have been exciting.'

'You're not wrong there.' Said Royer, 'but too much excitement can get a man killed. It's bad enough here and in

Caen and Le Havre. You know how rough it can get. It's worse now than when we were starting out.'

'Think he might get bored here Royer,' said Mouche, 'you think he'll remember why he left in the first place?'

'Perhaps he had enough excitement?' said Royer, 'I wouldn't blame him. It's bound to get to you after a while.'

'You never know,' said Mouche.

'He'll see us out to retirement, Moochy, you wait and see,' said Royer, 'I'd guess he's got a plan in mind.'

'I'll not be playing cards with him,' said Mouche, 'I'd likely lose my pension.'

'See Mouche, even you can learn from your mistakes.'

'Thanks, old friend.'

'Steady on. Don't start getting all sentimental. You'll want a kiss off me next Moochy.'

'Shut up!'

'You know what I think,' said Royer, leaning in conspiratorially, 'you know what this is all about?'

'What?'

'It's no secret is it,' said Royer, 'I think he's got an idea of what happened to his old man.'

'What?'

'Someone in Paris must have given him a clue. Stands to reason.'

'What reason?'

'Well, it doesn't have to be Paris,' said Royer.

'No, or he'd go there wouldn't he?'

Royer scratched his chin, 'True enough, and his old man has been gone for what, five years?'

'Six in March,' said Mouche, 'makes you think how fast the time goes.'

'That was some vanishing trick. Poof!' Royer waved his hands dramatically in the air, 'And he was gone. No trace. House all shut up and keys with the Notaire.'

'Maybe his new young wife did him in?' said Mouche, 'maybe he's still there under the flagstones in the cellar?'

'Perhaps she did Moochy, for all the hidden gold eh?'

'I suppose, with him being the commissaire it means he's in a good position to find out what happened?'

'Maybe Moochy, just maybe he already knows?'

'What? Like he was in on it?'

'Could be?'

'I don't know,' said Mouche, wiping the last of his coffee from his cup, 'what would be the point?'

Royer shrugged.

'Reckon I'm too old to care.'

'Didn't someone come looking for them?'

'Yeah, that horrible little Corsican fellow.'

'I seem to remember him being taller than you, Sarge.'

'Everyone's taller than me Moochy,' Royer scratched his head, 'comes from my mother being a Belgian.'

'He was offering a reward for information is what I heard,'

'And you know what they say about that?' Royer leaned in again to Mouche.

'What?'

'There's nothing like the prospect of a Corsican reward to make sure no one says a word.'

'How long was he here?' Mouche shuddered and peered into his empty coffee cup.

'About a week I suppose,' Royer took up scratching his chin again, 'didn't cause us any trouble.'

'I wondered what anyone would want with a retired magician?'

'Who knows eh? Old man Bassé had his airs and graces but before he was a big name in Paris he was with a travelling show,' said Royer, 'went all over the place, to Russia, to Istanbul, lots of places.'

'Do you think that's where he went?'

'Back to the circus?'

'Yeah,' said Mouche, 'going back to his beginnings.'

'Could be. Nothing much surprises me these days, Moochy.'

'Except for young Bassé coming back to Bayeux,' said Mouche.

'Except for that, yes.' Royer stretched and yawned. 'We've another new man in the station. The even younger Wimereux.

He doesn't look like he's even started thinking about shaving yet that boy. How is he getting on with Desnier?'

'Seems alright to me,' Mouche caught Royer's yawn, 'no complaints from either side.'

'Good.'

There was a knock on the canteen door.

'It's alright,' Royer called out, 'it's not private in here. Come on in.'

'Thank you, sir,' said Wimereux.

'Talk of the Devil,' said Royer, 'and he shall appear.'

'What do you mean sir?' said Wimereux.

'The sarge was just asking me about you,' said Mouche, 'How are you doing?'

'Yes, well thank you, sir.' His voice was steady and firm despite his youth.

'Good, glad to hear it young man,' said Royer. He looked the young constable up and down.

Desnier followed Wimereux into the room. A good half-dozen years separated the two policemen, but more besides. Desnier had come from a difficult stable.

'Good morning Sarge, morning Mouche. Another freezing morning then. Can't wait till Spring,' he said.

'I know,' said Royer, 'feels like January is the longest month. Every year it seems to get longer. It must be up to a hundred days long this year.'

'Feels like it,' nodded Mouche, 'the mayor should do something about it.'

Royer chuckled.

'There's a farmer's boy at the front desk who says he wants to speak to the man in charge,' said Desnier, 'that's you, Sarge, isn't it?'

'At the moment, yes,' said Royer, 'what does he want?'

'He smells awful,' said Desnier.

'Sounds like one of your relatives Mouche,' Royer chuckled.

'The only one that would marry you,' Mouche fired back, 'and she's got four legs too.'

'Now now,' said Royer, 'best I go and see.' He stood up with a groan, 'can't wait for the warmer weather. Gets in my bones does this cold.'

Wimereux poured a coffee for himself and one for Desnier. 'There was ice on the insides of the barracks windows this morning.'

'Keeps the drafts out Wims,' said Desnier, 'the wind can't get in if the holes are frozen solid.'

'My blanket was stiff too.'

'You'll get used to it. When I was on the farm, we had dirt floors. We only had stone by the front door,' said Desnier, 'Winter was great because there was less mud, so the barracks are luxury as far as I am concerned.'

'Would it hurt to light a fire?' Wimereux held his coffee cup in two hands letting the steam warm the end of his nose.

'It's not going to stay lit all night now is it Wims?' Desnier blew on his coffee before taking a sip.

'When I was new like you,' said Mouche, 'I was happy for the food and lodging.'

'I'm not complaining,' said Wimereux.

'Yes, you are,' said Desnier, 'most definitely.'

'Perhaps I'll get used to it?' said Wimereux.

'We could bring in some ladies to warm us up,' said Desnier, 'I know some that'll keep us like toast all night long.'

'Against the regulations I'm afraid,' said Mouche, 'you'd get sent away for that.'

'You have to be in the married quarters if you want better accommodation, Wims mate.' Said Desnier.

'Then I will have to get married,' said Wimereux.

'What? Just to keep warm?' Desnier laughed, 'You must be feeling the cold. Either that or it's affecting your sense.'

'Well, I was planning to get married one day,' said Wimereux.

'Who to?'

'I don't know Des. I haven't had the pleasure of meeting her yet.'

'I despair, Wims.'

'Do you have a girl Desnier?'

61

'Almost as many as old Mouche here,' said Desnier, 'a man with a moustache the size of his has to fight them off.'

'It's not my moustache the ladies want,' said Mouche.

'I don't know,' said Desnier, 'I'd be happy to lay money you have at least two beauties hidden in there right now.'

'Where?' said Mouche.

'In your moustache,' said Desnier.

Mouche laughed, 'It's too early in the morning for me Des'. I've only just finished my coffee and pipe.'

'That's what you need to do Wims,' said Desnier.

'What?'

'Cultivate your upper lip for the ladies.'

'But I can barely grow eyebrows.'

'What can we do?' Desnier sighed, 'You are hardly out of britches. How did you do it Mouche? How did you manage to raise such a fine beast under your nose? For our new man here?'

'I think I was born with it,' said Mouche.

'Monsieur and madame Mouche, congratulations, it's a moustache,' boomed Desnier, 'it would have been bigger than you. The midwife might have put you on the end of her broomstick to sweep up afterwards.'

'What are we doing today Desnier,' Wimereux cut in, desperate to change the subject.

'I don't know do I Wims? Right now, we are keeping warm,' said Desnier.

'The sarge will have something for you both I imagine,' said Mouche, getting to his feet. 'I'm just off to mind my own business.'

'Fair enough boss,' said Desnier, 'so Wims, got a wife in mind have you?'

'Sort of,' Wimereux studied the swirls in his coffee.

'Does she know?' Desnier peered across the top of his cup.

'Not yet,'

'Are you saving up for a love token? Got it all planned out?'

'Not really,'

'Okay, so let's see. Do I know the lucky lady?'

'I suppose you might.'

'You suppose?'

'Yes.'

'Is she your girlfriend?' Desnier raised his eyebrows.

'No,' said Wimereux.

'No?'

'At least, not yet.'

'Why not?'

'I haven't asked her,'

'I am guessing that you have at the very least, spoken to this woman?'

'Well.'

'You haven't have you, Wims?'

'I don't know.'

'What are we going to do with you?'

'It's difficult. I haven't had much of a chance really,'

'Let me help you out.'

'Would you?'

'I am the king of hearts Wimsy. Take my advice and you won't regret it.'

'What do I have to do?'

'First Wims, tell me, who is the lucky lady?'

'The baker's daughter.'

'What?' Desnier was incredulous.

'You know, the place on the corner behind the cathedral.'

'Yes, yes, I know who and where but Wims, oh dear,' he stifled a guffaw with his fist.

'What's the problem? Please don't say she is already married,' said Wimereux.

'No, not married as far as I know,' said Desnier, his shoulders beginning to shake.

'What then?'

'It's complicated,' Desnier gasped.

'How?'

'Let me put it this way. Could you, just as easily, fall in love with a different baker's daughter?'

'You think it's just the pastries?' Wimereux was insulted now.

'I will try again. Let me see,' Desnier frowned, then smiled as an idea struck him, 'How about the sarge sitting on the top table at your wedding?'

'But I'm not related to Sergeant Royer,' said Wims.

Desnier waited, silently counting off the seconds while he watched for the penny to drop. When he reached twenty, he realised the new boy needed an extra prod, 'Royer is her uncle. His brother is the baker. The sarge is in there every morning for his croissants and brioche.'

'That's not so bad is it?' said Wimereux.

'I don't know,' said Desnier.

'She is very beautiful, and the other morning our eyes met, and my face felt hot. I had to look away.'

'Do you even know her name Wims, eh?'

'No.'

'It's Brigitte,'

'Brigitte, such a beautiful name.'

'I suppose so Wims.'

'Is she promised to anyone?'

'I don't think so.'

'Perfect.'

'Not that you'd be the first to notice her.'

'What do you mean?'

'Royer knows we all go in there for our pastries. There is a steady stream of police uniforms in and out of that door all day. Everyone knows Brigitte and Brigitte knows everyone.'

'And?'

'And no one will speak to her because they are all scared of the sarge.'

'Even you?'

'Even me Wims. Any constable with a sensible head on his shoulders should be afraid of Sergeant Royer,' said Desnier, arms spread wide to encompass all of the Bayeux commissariat.

'Very true Constable Desnier,' said Royer as he burst into the canteen, 'now I want you both saddled up in five minutes flat. We have work to do.'

'What's up sir?' asked Wimereux.

'How many dead men have you seen in your lifetime boy?'

'None, sir.'

'Then you are in luck. Now move it.'

'First time for everything Wims,' said Desnier, 'you're in for a treat.'

'Shut up Desnier,' snapped Royer.

'Yes sir, sorry sir.'

Chapter Seven.

Royer was waiting for me at the front door of the commissariat.

'We have a dead man, sir,' he said, straight to the point.

'Good morning to you too Sergeant,' I said, saluting, then shaking his hand, 'where is it?'

'In a shack across the bridge from the Tire-Vite.'

'In sight of Madame Osment's place?'

'That's right sir.'

'Coincidence?'

'He doesn't look like her kind of customer to me, sir.'

'You've seen him?' I frowned, 'You should have called on me Sergeant.'

'Sorry sir, I was about to when you arrived here,' Royer looked at his boots, 'I was in early and met the farm boy when he came in with a message. I've got the new boy Wimereux out there with Desnier to keep guard until the doctor has seen him.'

'Very good then Royer, get someone to make sure Magpie is ready and pour me a coffee. It's too cold to walk anywhere else this morning.' I hoped I would quickly re-acclimatize to the Norman winters, but it would take time, and I regretted my tone with the Sergeant. He was a good man. Better than most.

Royer was quick with the coffee. I was in a hurry. Some say the dead can wait, that they have had their last appointment, but I found that if I did not get there first it could invite all kinds of trouble. In Paris, there were souvenir hunters, or rather pickpockets and common thieves who would strip a corpse as thoroughly as a peasant could pluck a chicken. I gulped the drink down and gradually felt myself warming through. I checked my desk for new paperwork. There was always more paperwork. I left it and went downstairs and out to the yard.

I decided that I should visit the mayor today as soon as possible. If I waited any longer it would be very rude.

Within ten minutes Royer had Magpie ready and waiting.

'I do like Magpie,' said Royer, 'she's a good horse.'

'She'll do quite well,' I said. I do not have a lot of expertise with horses, but Magpie was already proving tolerant of my poor handling, and I was able to enjoy her sure-footed ride. I admired the white flashes at her temples and again on her throat. A pretty horse too.

Royer rode beside me but kept his counsel, for which I was grateful. I cannot tolerate a *moulin a paroles*, people who talk too much and say nothing. The town was busy with preparations for tomorrow's market. Every Friday the wider communes came together in the main square and surrounding streets. It was traditionally the busiest part of the week for us with regular guests downstairs in our cells. I watched the city drift by. Some things had changed in the last decade. The same shop fronts remained with their familiar signs, but there was something of a new feeling to the place as if Bayeux had had a little lift. There was money coming into town, and that would bring change and new challenges for the old guard.

Villas and houses were being built along the roads radiating out into the countryside, bringing money into the mayor's coffers. It would forever be dwarfed by Caen, but Caen could not compete with Bayeux's cathedral, which towered over everything else in Normandy.

We passed a building site on the way to the old bridge. I caught the sound of workmen whistling as they loaded out materials onto the scaffold. It looked like it would be a pleasant part of town one day. The plots were well-spaced, and the boulevards had been kept wide.

After the mayor, I would pay a visit to the old house. The police service was not paying my hotel bill and I needed to hold on to the funds I had built up while I was away. I resolved I would chase out any lingering ghosts and sleep there tonight if I could manage it. There was an apartment at the commissariat that I could use but I could not imagine the circumstances which would force me into living above the shop, as it were.

We crossed the bridge by Madame Osment's ruinous bar. The construction work was continuing almost up to her back door.

I hoped that it would not be long before the sordid establishment would be swallowed up by new development.

Royer signalled for us to stop. We had arrived at a point almost at the city limits. Across a field dotted with Normandy cows was a low half-timbered building. It was surrounded by the wiry black whorls of brambles that covered half the structure like the web of a gigantic, demented spider.

The two constables were stamping their feet in the frost to keep warm and snapped to attention at our approach. I let them remain in position until I had dismounted.

'At ease,' I called, to their relief, and handed the reins of my horse to the younger man.

Royer led the way to a door leaning up against an opening. It was easy to see where the brambles had been trodden down for access. I cast about for any indication of whether there might have been a struggle, but the area looked like a herd of cows had been driven through it. There were no wolf tracks or other tell-tale signs of a predator.

'Has anyone been through the doorway yet?' I said.

'No sir, not even the farmer's boy,' said Royer, 'and we just looked in from here. You can see the man quite well enough from the outside. So much light comes in through the roof.'

'Good,' I said, and Royer stepped aside. I peered through the gloom. The cold weather meant that at least no flies were buzzing around. At last, a positive regarding the winter weather. If this were Guyana the air would have been thick with them. The body would have been invisible.

A shaft of light fell across the dirt floor and picked out a naked foot. As my eyes adjusted, more became clear. The man was laid out on his back with his arms thrown to his sides in a cruciform arrangement in the only clear space on the floor.

'First impressions are that he was dragged in and dropped as soon as he was in the door,' I said, 'one, maybe two people. He is a big man, our customer.'

He was well dressed apart from the fact that his shoes were missing. The immediate thought that struck me was Jean Mortain had also lost his shoes. I dismissed it immediately as a random factor. If there was a connection this was surely circumstantial.

'Was he killed for his shoes?' asked Royer.

'Maybe,' I said as I entered the shack, 'or perhaps he had started to get undressed before he was killed, which would confirm the suspicion that he may have been killed somewhere else before being brought here.'

'Who takes their shoes off first?' said Royer.

'Someone about to remove their trousers Sergeant,' I said.

'I start at the top and work down,' said Royer.

'Interesting,' I said.

'Thank you, sir.'

'Not you Royer,' I said, 'get your boys to check the field for a pair of socks.'

'Pardon?'

'See the victim's heels where they have been scratched by brambles?'

'Yes, sir.'

'My guess is he was dragged across the field. He's a big man and he would be difficult to move to this vagabond's mausoleum.'

'I will instruct them right away.'

'If they find the socks, they must not touch them.'

'Understood sir.'

I stepped over the body, careful to place my feet in case I should destroy any essential sign. I studied the man's face. Someone had taken the trouble to close his eyes. The expression on the face was quite neutral. His hair was untidy but well-kept along with his fine moustache. It was clear he attended the barber shop regularly.

I noticed his coat was of a good cut as I bent over him to inspect his pockets. I gave the lapel of his coat a brief tug and it came away slowly, stuck hard as it was with blood. I pulled harder and saw where the wound had been made. There was a ragged tear in the material, which suggested either a small-bore gun or a stab wound. There was insufficient light to see whether there was staining from a firearm. I would leave that detail to the doctor.

I felt the other lapel. It came away easily and I was able to fish in an inside pocket. There was no wallet, but I did find a small square of paper. It was a ticket stub from the theatre, from last weekend, a comic farce. So, he had been in town for at least a week. Had he been staying at the Hotel de Ville I might have noticed this tall, distinguished figure. Judging by his tailoring he was not one for the inns so that just left the Hotel du Theatre. I would have to visit both.

A maker's mark inside the coat gave Marseille as the location of his tailor, which would help when asking after missing hotel guests. There was nothing else to aid me here. I patted his other pockets. No wallet, no watch, nothing else to help with identification. I peered down at his face. There were indentations on either side of the bridge of his nose. He had worn spectacles.

'At the end of a long day,' I mused aloud, 'our victim returns to a hotel room. His feet are hurting from walking, standing or perhaps he has been busy sightseeing? Perhaps he has been lecturing or performing some service on his feet all day? He empties his pockets, removes his spectacles, takes off his shoes then someone puts a knife in him and then drags him out of town.'

'Why would they do that?' asked a gentleman in the doorway.

'I know, it makes no sense yet,' I said, 'but good morning sir, I assume you are the doctor?'

'Doctor Richelieu at your service,' he put out a gloved hand, 'I take it you are Hautefort's replacement?'

'Indeed, Inspector Bassé,' I said.

'Good to meet you,' said the doctor.

We shook hands across the dead man's body, then the doctor bent down for a closer inspection.

'Have you finished here Inspector?' he asked.

'Yes, Doctor. I do not believe he was killed here. Looks like he was murdered elsewhere then dumped here in a poor attempt at concealment,' I said, 'With the river still frozen and the ground as solid as rock I suppose there was little alternative.'

'Neat job,' muttered the doctor, 'looks like a single blow from behind and directly through the heart. He has most likely been here a day or two. They stay fresher for longer this time of year. I will know more once we get him back.'

'How long?' I asked.

'Were his eyes closed when you arrived Inspector?' he said.

'Yes, of course. I checked his pockets but otherwise, he remained untouched.'

'Why would they close his eyes, do you think?' The doctor furrowed his brow.

'It's likely the killer had a personal relationship with the victim. I will find out eventually.' I said, 'I usually do.'

'I admire your confidence, young man.' The doctor smiled up at me.

'I am finished here,' I said, 'so you can have him taken away. Let me know what you find as soon as you are able.'

'Of course. Good luck.' He said.

'Thank you, Doctor.' I left the godforsaken shack and stepped out into the frost-covered field. The doctor's porters stood at the ready with a stretcher for the deceased. Beyond them, my gendarmes waited in a huddle in the field halfway to the lane. When I caught up to my men, I saw they had found a sock.

'You were right sir,' said Royer, 'and there are tracks too where whoever was carrying or dragging him had to dig their heels in.'

I inspected the cast-off garment and the divots in the cold, hard earth.

'Getting the dead man to this place was hard work by the looks of it,' I was thinking out loud, 'so our suspect is likely not used to physical labour.'

'The fellow's not that big,' said Royer, 'but still, I might have a little trouble on my own. You wonder why they didn't just drop him in the river?'

'Indeed,' I said, 'but it does remain frozen solid. It looks to me like either our customer was meant to be discovered, or the killers ran out of time before they could dispose of him properly. I also think we are looking for more than one villain in this case.'

'What shall we do with this sock?' said Royer.

I shuddered, but not with the cold. Jean Mortain's shoes and stockings had been missing when he was found abandoned in the river not half a kilometre from here. Did it matter? Was there a link? My instinct told me it was nothing, but still, a doubt remained. I shook my head. I would discount nothing, but what I wanted were facts more than anything.

'Put it with the corpse. The relatives, if he has any, might want it back,' I said, 'see how it is half rolled up? That tells me it came off on its own as his feet were dragged across the ground.'

'It's full of dirt and frost,' said Royer, picking it up from its resting place.

'Thank you, Royer,' I said, 'now stay on hand to help the doctor and then secure the shack in case we need to revisit. Tell the farmer and his boy that no one is to enter until we say so.'

'Very good, sir.'

'I need to pay a visit to the Hotel du Theatre with one of these two constables. Choose for me, Sergeant.'

'Desnier will accompany you, sir,' said Royer.

Chapter Eight.

The Hotel du Theatre was one of those older buildings which had had many various functions over the years. A hotel was its current raison d'etre and as such it looked reasonably suited. The entrance had been enlarged and enhanced with a small colonnaded portico to add a sense of drama.

To either side were set a table and two chairs for the audience, although I suspect there were few takers at this time of year. Still, they had been recently polished, and the cobbles swept but they were more an invitation to imagine warmer times.

I mounted the steps with my constable and found myself in a brightly lit foyer with a gleaming front desk, behind which sat an equally well-looked-after gentleman. If he was surprised or otherwise disturbed by the arrival of the police. it was impossible to tell. He was quite clearly a professional concierge above all.

'Bonjour Monsieur,' I said, 'allow me to introduce myself. I am Inspector Bassé of the Bayeux Police, and I am currently investigating the murder of a man whom I suspect may well have been staying here at your hotel.'

'Oh dear Inspector, how awful,' he stood and offered his hand, 'I am Paul Nolet. This is my hotel. I do hope your suspicions are unfounded, but I am completely at your service.'

We shook hands, and then Nolet made a show of running his finger down a page of a thick ledger that lay open on the desk.

'Do you have a name?' he said, his finger pausing momentarily on the paper.

'No. I was hoping to find that out here.' I said, 'Are any of your guests absent at the moment?'

'Not as far as I am aware Inspector, but discretion is our watchword here. We respect the privacy of our guests, and they appreciate that part of our service,' he studied the ledger, 'and it is not unknown for some of our more artistic residents to keep unusual hours.'

'But you keep records like all good businesses?' I watched him as he inspected his list.

'Of course, sir,' his finger arrived at the bottom of the page, 'and I can confirm that everyone is accounted for.' He tapped the ledger with the index finger on his right hand.

'How about two days ago? Did anyone leave early, change their booking?' I tried to catch his eye, but he stared resolutely at the book.

'Let me check sir. People come and go all the time.' He said, turning the page.

'Of course,' I said, 'I understand.'

'Three guests left the day before yesterday, Tuesday,' Nolet's brow furrowed, 'Monsieur and Madame Richard and Monsieur Sabat.'

'This Sabat, was he a big gentleman?' I said.

'I suppose he was quite tall, as I recall.' Nolet looked up at last. I finally caught his gaze and held it.

'From the south perhaps?' I said, 'Did he have an accent?'

'Yes, I believe so.' Nolet looked away again, down at the lines of cursive script traced across his ledger.

'Marseille, perchance?' I pushed it.

'Let me check sir,' Nolet consulted another dossier, 'Absolutely right sir. Did you know the gentleman?'

'Did your guest leave anything behind?' I ignored his question.

'Not that I am aware of,' said Nolet, making a show of examining more paperwork.

'When did you last see him?' I said.

'Monday, I believe,' said Nolet.

'And how was he?'

'The same, jovial as always,' Nolet smiled at the memory, 'he was a salesman and visited quite regularly. When men like him travel for work, they like stability, the routine of staying somewhere familiar.'

I noticed the concierge had a clean bandage on his left hand.

'You have an injury, Monsieur Nolet?'

'This?' He held up his hand, 'A small thing. A burn. Sometimes I help in the kitchen, but I am afraid I am too clumsy to be allowed to help too often.'

'Is the hotel full today?' I said.

'Almost,'

'Has monsieur Sabat's room been re-let?' The question took Nolet by surprise.

'Not yet.' He looked startled as a hare.

'Good. I would like to see it if you don't mind.'

'Certainly, Inspector,' the concierge turned to his keyboard and made a show of checking and rechecking the keys. He turned back to me with a pained expression on his face. 'I am afraid the key does not appear to be here sir. It is probably out with housekeeping.'

'You do not have a master key?'

'I do apologise sir. Our hotel is not as modern as some.' He gave me a pained expression.

'And your housekeeper?'

'She will return this afternoon.' Nolet folded his hands together on the ledger.

'Then so will I. Good day Monsieur,' I said, 'but make sure no one enters the room until I return.'

'As you wish, inspector,' said Nolet.

When I was back on the pavement with my constable, I pulled Desnier to one side and gave him instructions for Royer. I watched him go, leading Magpie. In the centre of town, every important building is within easy walking distance.

If my instinct was right, we had little time to lose. Behind the concierge, there was a door to a back office, and I had seen quite clearly a large pair of shoes balanced atop a suitcase. Perhaps it was something, perhaps it was nothing, but a good policeman can never ignore his gut. Besides, the concierge had referred to Sabat in the past tense, which meant that Nolet knew more than he was letting on and was probably covering for someone at the very least. A second interview at the commissariat would test his discretion a little more, it did tend to loosen tongues, but right now I needed to pay a visit to the mayor's office. I had passed it by on the way to and from my own office for two days and it could not wait any longer.

Mayor Gevrol and Inspector Hautefort had never been the best of friends. Royer had already warned me that my predecessor saw Gevrol as a political backward step with his royalist leanings, while the mayor thought the former inspector was past his prime. Now was the time for a fresh start and I was determined to maintain a professional relationship with the man.

I like progress and hope to change Bayeux for the better. I want to bring fresh thinking into the commissariat while respecting the experience and wisdom that existed in some of the old guard. Paris had been an ossuary for progressive policing while Cayenne had been too creative for my taste. Things are hopefully moving on, but I am wary of the politicians talking about reform for the sake of it. France is a revolutionary nation by nature, but some things do not benefit from being turned upside down.

The doors to the council offices were opened every day at nine. I arrived no more than five minutes later and spent my first ten minutes observing the satisfying quiet efficiency of the French state at the civic level. It was busy with purposeful citizens seeking permissions and officials turning the wheels of the legislative machine.

The mayor had to rubberstamp my appointment. He may have already done so if he was keen to replace Hautefort. I made my presence known at reception and was called upstairs to wait outside Gevrol's office. I did not have to wait long.

'Inspector Bassé,' cried the mayor as he burst out of his door. He was a tall man, a native of Bayeux with an aristocratic Normandaise hauteur. He wore a beard in a knightly cruciform fashion, so favoured by those who fancied they had family links with le Conqueror.

We shook hands. He clasped mine with both of his and held on for a little longer than I felt was polite.

'Come into my office,' he waved me toward the door.

'Yes, sir.'

And what an office it was. In pride of place over a grand marble fireplace was an oil painting of the mayor in armour, clasping the flag of Normandy, and sitting atop a magnificent white Percheron. He certainly looked the part, and it gave off a very strong impression of baronial authority. I could not help but stare.

'Do you like it?' he asked, preening.

I nodded. 'A very good likeness sir. You must be very pleased with it.'

'My gift to the city,' he said and sat down, indicating that I should do the same, 'I think you will find me a generous man with some understanding of our hometown and its various iniquities. However, Bayeux is, in the main, a peaceful and prosperous place with no serious problems Inspector. You will find the normal difficulties and distractions that come with market day and with travelling shows, but we have never had any real scandal.'

'I am glad to hear that sir,' I said.

'Apart from that unfortunate business with your father,' he fixed me with a hard look.

'I understand your concern sir, but it was some time ago and I can assure you, it will not distract me from my duty to the people of the city.' I said, 'My concern is the present and the future, not the past. I understand the matter was investigated by my predecessor and the dossier has since been closed.'

'Correct Inspector,' his face softened, 'and how have your first days been?'

'Eventful sir. A funeral for an old friend yesterday and this morning a murder.' I said. I could not put honey on it. I was not going to soft-soap the mayor on anything.

'A murder? Who?' Gevrol was alarmed.

'A man was discovered on the city limits this morning. I believe he might be a travelling salesman from Marseille although, as you can appreciate, the investigation is in its early stages at the moment.' I said.

'We haven't murdered an outsider for years,' Gevrol frowned, 'this is the last thing we need. You need to make an arrest as soon as possible. Get the case closed as quickly, and quietly as you can.'

'There may be an arrest quite soon sir, but it could be a little longer before we have enough evidence for the investigating magistrate.'

'Of course, Bassé. We have kept all the killings within our own circle up to now. You know the sort, muggings, family rows, business fallouts,' his frown deepened, 'but people need to know that Bayeux is a safe place to visit.'

'Of course, sir,' I said.

'Murders are bad for business,'

'Indeed sir.'

'Judge Tanquerel will help with warrants. Judge Dampier is due to retire soon so may be less interested. I will leave that up to you.' His frown was gone, replaced with a thoroughly neutral, unreadable expression.

'Thank you, sir,' I said, realising the interview was over.

'You may go Bassé,' the mayor dismissed me with a brusque wave of his hand, as if annoyed I had brought a murder inquiry through his door at our first meeting. I stood, nodded, and marched to the door. I could hardly blame the fellow.

'Welcome to my city Inspector,' he muttered to my back.

His city, I thought to myself as I made my way out to the square. I wondered what his city looked like. I doubted whether it looked like mine.

I called on the Judge at the Palais de Justice. He was a late riser and would not be in till after eleven. I left a message for him confirming my requirement for a warrant to search the Hotel du Theatre and then made my way to the old house. Madame Langlois was expecting me at half past ten and it was almost that time already.

I was late but the housekeeper had let herself in and lit a fire in the kitchen. The pale smoke rose above the chimney, and I felt a lump rise in my throat. I stood on the pavement for a minute and took it all in. The square had not changed that much since I had been away. I looked up at the old family home, the three-storey townhouse that had been the end of the line for our travelling days. The final step, or so we thought.

The courtyard had sprouted weeds, a willow by the front gate, and a buddleia pushing out between the flagstones, and there was an ivy creeping up the round tower built to house a staircase. My father had wanted to make the house a chateau. It embarrassed me at the time, but now it just looked like home.

There had been good times in the house and sad times of course, but soon there would be different times. It was a big house for one man to inhabit. I had no illusions or, I thought, no emotional tie to the ancient stone and mortar, and it was odd walking through the familiar front door again, feeling the old emotions rushing down the hall to meet me.

When I imagined my return, it was never like this, never to a quiet uninhabited place. I had always expected to find my father engrossed in some new invention, another grand illusion that he would sell on to the up-and-coming new cohort of younger magicians. Father had always been an engineer and a craftsman first and foremost, delighting in the invention of the miraculous.

I think his dream was for me to follow his passion for engineering and maybe create something more permanent, more lasting than an evening's entertainment. It was my destiny to do something else. I think I disappointed him, but I would rather that than lead a life I could not believe in.

I heard Madame Langlois at work in the kitchen before I saw her, and it was as if I had slipped back in time. I listened for my father, and then with a lump in my throat I waited for my mother's call. Neither sound came and so I ventured deeper into the house. My house.

'Monsieur?' Madame Langlois was the niece of my father's former housekeeper and these days she did not need to live in and in fact, she was able to look after more than one household. This was ideal for me as I intended to take the old servant's quarters in the South wing for myself. It was convenient for the kitchen and had a separate entrance that gave onto the courtyard and made use of the spiral stair in the tower.

The rest of the old townhouse held the story of my father's disappearance. A story I had a mind to unravel if I could find the time and make the effort required.

'Madame Langlois, good day,' I called out, 'thank you for your hard work.'

'It is nothing, sir,' she said, 'I have put some provisions in your cupboards and made up your old bed here in the servant's quarters as you asked.'

'Thank you. I am sure I will be very comfortable here.'

My father had spared no expense in renovating the old place twenty years ago. The plumbing worked well and, though I was a little wary of them, the gas lamps gave an excellent light. An engineer had been engaged on my behalf by the Notaire to check everything thoroughly and make any repairs, as necessary.

'Madame,' I said, 'I understand that the housekeepers in the city know what happens behind closed doors.'

'Yes sir, but rest assured that we are very discreet,' she said.

'Of course, I appreciate that, but can you tell me who runs the housekeeping at the Hotel du Theatre?' I made a show of inspecting my new rooms. The place was spotless and quite warm.

'That would be Madame Omer,' she said, 'she is rather fierce but fair to those of us who work for her.'

'Glad to hear it. Have you seen her recently?' I said. I looked out of the front window at the overgrown yard. Another job.

'Of course,' she said, 'yesterday afternoon.'

'How was she?'

'The same as always. Why sir? Has something happened to her?'

'What? No, not that I know of,' I said, 'I was simply interested in taking a room for a visitor from Paris.'

'Well, I am sure the Hotel de Ville might be more proper for Parisian tastes sir.'

'Indeed, I thought so too,' I said, 'but I have been staying there myself this week, so I was not sure it was quite right.'

'I shouldn't say but Madame Omer has had a difficult week this week with noisy guests leaving a mess. If your guest likes their sleep, I should certainly recommend the Hotel de Ville.'

'Poor Madame Omer,' I sympathised.

'She had one guest up and disappear the other day. Left blood all over the sheets. A terrible mess. She thinks he must have fled in shame.'

'You have convinced me Madame Langlois. The Hotel de Ville it shall be.' I clapped my hands.

'You won't say anything will you?'

'To Madame Omer? Of course not, now about our contract.'

The paperwork was straightforward, and I agreed and signed it without hesitation, looking forward to my first night at home in Bayeux.

Chapter Nine.

At the commissariat, Royer confirmed he had concierge Paul Nolet secured in our donjon. I had him moved to an office for an interview and called for our stenographer. I studied Nolet through the small window in the door. He did not look as in possession of himself as he had done at the hotel earlier. It was clear he had not been sleeping well and a night in the cells tonight would not be much help to him either.

The stenographer arrived with his notebook and in we went. Royer stood by the door.

'We meet again, Monsieur Nolet,' I said, 'I imagine you are aware of why you are here?'

Nolet said nothing and did not move a muscle. His hands rested in his lap, and he stared straight ahead. He looked stunned.

'I am expecting to have to charge you with the perpetration of a criminal act. The level of your cooperation will decide the severity of the consequences. Do you understand?'

He nodded.

'This is a preliminary interview. Counsel will be appointed for you should you request it,' I said. Nolet shook his head. 'For the record I need you to state your name, age and residence please.'

'Paul Nolet, thirty-eight and I live at the Hotel du Theatre, Grand Rue, Bayeux.' He spoke in a low monotone without emotion and appeared resigned to whatever fate awaited him.

'Thank you, Monsieur. Now, I would like you to tell me how you knew the deceased, currently identified as Henri Sabat,' I looked at my notes, 'resident of Eighteen Rue des Marais, Marseilles?'

'He was a guest at the hotel,' said Nolet.

'How long had he been staying with you?'

'About three weeks.'

'Did you see the gentleman every day?'

'Most days. He would travel the north coast from Cherbourg to Le Havre. The monsieur has been coming to us every January for some years now.' Nolet half smiled. This concierge was proud of his role in securing repeat business during the low season.

'When did you see him last?'

'I saw him on Monday evening. He was going out to see friends.' Nolet's confidence was growing.

I felt like Nolet had been rehearsing answers in his head, anticipating the questions he might face. He knew something and was either protecting himself or someone else. I would have to work harder to break through his finely honed concierge's discretion.

'That was the last time you saw Monsieur Sabat alive?'

'Yes,' he nodded.

'You didn't see him when he left the next morning?' I spoke as casually as I could.

'No.' A small hesitation.

'Is that because he left the building rather earlier than usual, before most of the staff were at work?'

No answer. Nolet continued to stare but now his gaze was downcast, and his hands twitched in his lap.

'I don't know,' he said, 'I don't know anything.'

'Monsieur Nolet, I have to inform you that a warrant has been sought from the Judge to enable a thorough search of the Hotel du Theatre, including Monsieur Sabat's hotel room. Regardless of your discretion, we shall discover everything in due course. It is what we do.

'While you think on that let me ask you another question. The gentleman was discovered not too far from a bridge over a river where another dead man was discovered just a few days ago.

'Both men within walking distance of the public drinking house of Madame Osment. When I last spoke to the lady, she mentioned your hotel and a young man who, she says, works there. Now I do not like to believe in that sort of coincidence. In my experience they never, ever happen.'

Nolet was beginning to sweat. 'We have a business relationship, that's all,' he said, 'she provides a service we can rely on at the hotel. She's very discreet.'

'Of course, she is,' I said, 'when she is speaking to you. But I understand that quite a bit of business goes in and out of the back door at the Hotel du Theatre does it not?'

Nolet shrugged.

'Don't tell me you don't know who is coming or going?' I put down my pen and shook my head.

'I do,' said Nolet, 'I do, but I don't want to embarrass anyone.'

'Nolet, a man is lying dead at the doctor's office so I will knock on every door in the hotel if I have to until I get some answers.' I said, 'Then I will call on all of Madame Osment's staff too.'

'You would do that?' He said.

'I would Nolet,' I smiled at him, 'perhaps I would put them in a carriage and bring them all down here and sit them in the chair you are sitting in, one by one.'

'No.'

'I will be paying a visit to the Judge later, the man who will be investigating this murder and prosecuting the case,' I said.

I kept quiet for a moment letting the nightmare scenario sink in. He picked at the bandage on his hand.

'How did you cut yourself, Paul?' I asked.

'A knife. It's nothing,' said Nolet.

'A particularly hot knife?' I said.

'Pardon?'

'This morning, at the hotel, you told me you had burned yourself in the kitchen.'

'Oh yes, that's right, but I cut myself too.'

'Do you have many accidents, Nolet?'

'Yes, I mean no. I don't know.'

'The knife that did for Monsieur Sabat was very sharp. Something a hotel chef might use to cut meat.'

Nolet raised his eyes to mine.

'Look, Nolet. I know you know what happened,' I said, 'I understand it's difficult. I am willing to bet you have never had to deal with a situation like this before. Am I right?'

He sat motionless in the chair. It was as if he had been defeated by life. For a moment I felt sorry for him, but the moment passed. Was Paul Nolet a hardened criminal or a mark for a bigger concern, I wondered.

'I am also willing to bet that if we removed your bandage from your left hand, we would not find a burn, but a stab wound, likely from the same knife that took the gentleman's life.'

Nolet shrugged.

'I will call the doctor to come and attend to your wound when we have finished here, but before then I am going to tell you what I think happened.

'I understand your aversion to scandal, your need to keep up a good impression. You are not alone. The mayor wants Bayeux to be seen as a safe, modern, and prosperous city too. On the other hand, you want to keep your guests happy so you do whatever you can, even if what you do is sometimes not morally right and proper in the eyes of wider society.

'I am not saying that what you do for your clients is criminal, but you walk a narrow path, sir.

'On Monday night, your guest, Henri Sabat, returns in the middle of the night with an unsuitable person. Things get somewhat out of hand, and you are called upon by other guests to quieten things down. When you get to Sabat's room an argument ensues and somehow you find yourself pushing a blade between the gentleman's ribs.'

'No,' shouted Nolet, 'that's not how it went at all.'

'Then please Nolet, help my understanding.'

'He was probably already dead when I was called by Doctor Vallet from the room below about the noise. I went and knocked and when I got no reply, I let myself in and found the gentleman on the floor with a knife in his back.

'I pulled it out because I thought it might make him better. I suppose I went a little crazy.'

'What happened next, Nolet?' A look at Jacques the stenographer told me he was keeping up.

'I rolled him over and saw he was dead. My next thought was how he could not possibly stay here,' said Nolet, 'I had to get him out, clean up the room, and make it all go away.'

'Did you see anyone else, anyone at all?' I said.

'No, no one.'

'I see, and so you took it upon yourself to drag the recently deceased gentleman down the back stairs and out into the yard all on your own. Then load him on the back of a cart, without disturbing any of your guests?'

'Yes,' he nodded vigorously.

'And at no time did any of your staff come and investigate the noise?'

'What noise?'

'Monsieur Nolet, forgive me, but I do not see that you are built for heavy labour and our Henri Sabat, as we know, was not a small man.' I said, 'We know you have a night manager. Where was he that night?'

'I was alone, all the time.' Said Nolet, 'Chevrolet had a night off, so I was covering his shift. There was nobody else in the hotel who could be of any help to me.'

'Very well Nolet,' I shook my head, 'what happened next?'

'After I hid him on the cart I went back and cleaned up the room as best I could.'

'But still, your housekeeping staff complained that there was blood on his sheets.'

'How did you know?'

'It is my job to know these things, Nolet. As I have said before, we will learn everything in due course.' I stretched my legs under the desk, 'What I would like to discover is why you went to such heroic lengths to get rid of the body of a man you say you did not kill.'

'It was for the hotel.' He raised his hands and made a face that said, 'Isn't it obvious?'

'For the hotel? Not for the sake of some third party?'

'No.'

I closed my eyes and tried to imagine this small, neat little man dragging the giant Sabat silently through the hotel. I suppose that in a crisis we do sometimes discover untapped strength, but I could not convince myself. I was sure he must have had help.

He was beginning to try my patience, so I took a moment before I asked him anything else, letting him stew like an Englishman's tea, making him realise his answers were being treated with some thought.

'I am having difficulty with the inconsistencies in your answers, monsieur, and I think I might get better answers from your guests. Someone must have seen or heard something?'

'No,' he sighed, 'it would have been very bad for the hotel to have had a murder so I thought I should take him far away so the murder would look like it happened somewhere else.'

'What?'

'Who can sleep in a room where a man was stabbed to death?'

'Monsieur Nolet,' I said, 'what did you do with the murder weapon?'

'The knife I took out of his back, is wrapped in a shirt.'

'And I believe the gentleman's belongings are safely stowed in your office?'

'Yes, in my office Inspector. How did you know?'

'You made no attempt to hide them. I saw the case with the shoes balanced on top. I thought it curious, having just seen a barefoot corpse. Like I said before. I don't believe in coincidence.'

I glanced over at Royer. He seemed to be enjoying himself.

'When you collected Henri Sabat's things did you notice whether anything was missing Nolet?'

'His money belt was empty, and his wallet was gone, but I expect he had been at the card table.'

'I see,'

'But I have a sum of money in the hotel safe for him.'

'Of course, you do monsieur concierge, and I suppose it is enough to spark some interest?'

'A few hundred francs.'

'Enough to pay the cleaning bill and more besides. Well,' I paused for effect, 'this could make the mayor very happy indeed. It doesn't look good for you, but it looks incredibly good for me.'

'What do you mean?' Nolet was sweating. I had him imagining the rope or deportation.

'The city is more important than one man and our mayor understands that very well. You had the opportunity and motive and have admitted to removing the body and the victim's possessions. There is no jury that would not send you down.'

'But he was already dead,' protested Nolet.

'As you say, but you have caused so many problems by not coming straight to the commissariat as soon as you found him.'

'I panicked. I'm sorry, I didn't want the hotel to be shut down.' He was gripping the edge of the table now.

'In the absence of any other suspect at this time I am afraid we are going to have to detain you here on a charge of murder and concealment of a body.'

'What will happen to me?'

'Are your affairs in order?'

'Yes, of course.'

'Good. We will take care of you,' I said, 'give you some time to think. See if you can remember anything that might help you?' I looked up at Royer, 'The interview is over, Sergeant, please return our guest to the cells.'

'Very good sir,' said Royer.

'But I promise you it wasn't me,' said Nolet.

'They all say that,' said Royer, leading him away.

I could not quite believe Nolet had killed Sabat but the evidence against him was enough to see him found guilty. I could do worse in my first week in control of the Bayeux gendarmerie than catch a murderer. It would cement my place with the mayor, but it would not be right. I needed to go back to the hotel, search the room, and go through Sabat's things. Nolet was clearly out of his depth, mixed up in business he wasn't used to. The killer was still at large.

*

I returned to the Hotel du Theatre with Royer, Desnier, and Wimereux after lunch. Night manager Chevrolet was at the front desk in place of Nolet.

I had Royer begin to take statements from the staff while Chevrolet opened up the room for me. I stepped in with care but could see immediately where Nolet had scrubbed at the floorboards. The windows and shutters were all fastened tight against the cold. No trace of blood on the curtains, the walls, or the mattress. I guessed the bedsheets had been used to wipe up the mess. There was a faint discolouration to the boards. I crouched down on my haunches to get a closer look. A glint of silver caught my eye. Embedded in the wood was a thin slice of metal. I took out my penknife and began digging. After a few seconds, it popped out. The tip of a knife blade.

Sabat had fallen with such force from a blade driven into his back it must have pinioned him like some great beetle. It would have sounded like a thunderclap. No wonder Doctor Vallet had been roused. It should have woken the entire street.

I took the blade tip and wrapped it in a handkerchief. Under the bed, I found Sabat's wallet. I got on my knees to reach it. It was clean. No blood on the leather. Inside were about two hundred francs and some sou plus a note on some rather fine paper. It was written in a very neat hand and was an invitation to play cards with a certain Monsieur Loup. *Who plays cards with a man whose name translates as wolf?* I could hardly imagine how badly that could turn out.

I looked in the drawer in the bedside cabinet. There was a pack of cards, mid-range, with a reasonable bicycle print, not well used. Also, a creased postcard of an actress in a state of some undress, a pamphlet from the theatre, and a journal. There was a faded studio daguerreotype tucked inside the journal too. A picture of a handsome young woman. On the back the name 'Alita' and a date, August 15, 1882, Ascension Day. Sometimes the hottest day of the year in France. At last, something that might give up some detail on the life of this man.

I discovered his home address in Marseille written on the inside cover of a notebook. *In case he ever forgot it*. Why else would someone write their home address in their journal? Perhaps that was normal?

There were regular entries with names and places, Caen, Cherbourg, St. Malo, just as Nolet had said there would be. In between I noticed the words *Le Loup*. It seems he would visit this place or person every Monday. I made a mental note to find out what and where this was.

I could see no more of any interest in the journal. He was moving on to Picardy in February and then to Burgundy in March, returning to Marseilles in time for Easter. Home for the holiday. It must be like being part of a travelling show, a solo act putting on a spectacle in a different town to a new audience every month. But without the community travelling alongside it must have been a lonely way to live, with the dull trades of a small-town concierge standing in for true friendship. He had to have been a resilient character this Sabat.

The more I saw of other people's lives and the choices they made the happier I was to be a policeman.

Chapter Ten.

It was still early in the afternoon. Too early for any respectable person to be playing cards for money, but for many people, card playing is anything but a respectable pastime. I had been directed out to the Rue du Mer, to look out for the sign of the wolf hanging from a building on the corner of the street.

The light was fading when I finally came upon the place. The sign was small, just a single handspan square. In a blue circle, a wolf walked upon its hind legs, in one forepaw it held a club and in the other a shield. Its mouth was open in a broad tooth-filled leer while at its feet a royal peacock kept it company.

I shuddered. The image conjured up ancient fears.

I looked away from the sign of the wolf, shaking off the memory, the old family stories that I had some difficulty believing were true. As I did so I saw a door open onto the side road and two men half ran, half fell into the road.

'If I see you again, I will be the last thing you ever see,' roared an extraordinarily large man. He filled the doorway with his shoulders, and he had the neck of a bull. The two men scrambled to their feet and fled past me, not daring to look behind them. The giant caught my eye and briefly flashed a bright white smile at me.

'Commissaire,' he growled, 'my master said to look out for you.'

Loup's guardian stood aside and waved me in through the door. I was taken somewhat aback at how fast news travelled these days, and that a man appeared to recognize me so readily. His acute nose for the gendarmerie put me on alert that this man was definitely of the criminal class.

'Good afternoon sir,' I said, while alarms went off somewhere inside my head, but I held out my hand and we shook politely. His grip, which could surely crush a windpipe with ease, was firm but brief.

Inside there was a strong aroma of coffee and tobacco and it was warm with coals glowing in a fireplace.

'I am Mistretta, Loup's man who takes care of things. I throw out the rubbish as you saw,' he hesitated, 'I am sorry you had to see that. We don't get rubbish here often.'

'I understand,' I said.

'As I said, Monsieur Loup was expecting you to pay him a visit. If you could be so kind as to wait here for a moment, I shall let him know you have arrived.'

'No need to keep the Commissaire waiting,' came a voice from behind the giant.

'Monsieur,' said Mistretta, and stood to one side, revealing a well-dressed gentleman in his mid-thirties, sporting a pointed goatee and a smile as wide as his forest dwelling namesake.

'I am Loup,' he introduced himself and extended a gloved hand to me.

'Bonjour Monsieur Loup,' I said, taking a hand as limp and lifeless as Mistretta's was urgent.

'Commissaire, the pleasure is all mine. Are you here on business, or for entertainment?' Loup's smile never wavered. He was the complete professional host.

'I am sorry to say that I am here on business only.' I studied his face for a reaction, but he remained serene.

'That is a pity, for I understand you are a somewhat formidable player.' Loup winked.

'Don't believe everything you hear, Monsieur,' I said.

'Oh, I don't,' said Loup, 'I like to see for myself. Perhaps you would be able to play on another occasion once you have had time to settle in?'

'Perhaps, but for this visit, I would like a few minutes of your time to ask some questions.'

'Of course, and we will use my private salon.' Loup waved a hand at his man.

Mistretta pushed a panel next to a floor-length gold-framed mirror. The mirror sprang out into the hallway on hinges, revealing a comfortably appointed room with tall windows and a glowing fire in the hearth.

'Bring us coffee Mistretta,' Loup commanded, 'the South American beans.'

I followed Loup into his private room. It was hung with paintings of farmyards and fields and decorated with dark wood panels. The windows let in a huge amount of light, but the room still felt dark.

'Please take a seat Commissaire, Mistretta won't be long. There is always coffee being made.'

'Thank you,' I said, 'now I have come to you as I am investigating the death of one of your customers.'

'I'm sorry to hear that.' Loup lost his grin.

'Did you not already know the purpose of my visit?'

'I confess I did try and find that out. Had I another day I'm sure I would have discovered your purpose, sir.'

'Monsieur Henri Sabat,' I said, 'according to his diary he was here on Monday night.'

'He was here, that's right, and now the poor fellow is dead you say?'

'Yes.'

'That is a shame. He was a good customer, classy,' Loup grinned, 'not such a great card player but he was always good-natured and seemed to enjoy himself.'

'I see,' I said, 'and did you speak to him on Monday?'

'Absolutely. We had an hour or so at the table together. I like to play. I like to think I am a better, more skilled player than I am, so it was always a pleasure to play a man so easily impressed by my limited abilities.'

'How was he?'

'His usual amiable self,' Loup showed all his teeth, 'happy for me to take his money.'

'Did he upset anyone?'

'Henri was never a man to make enemies for himself. He was a salesman. A professional. Everyone he met was a prospect or could lead him to one. My establishment served as a meeting place where he could fish for new clients and entertain old ones.'

The secret door opened again and Mistretta appeared with cups and a coffee pot.

'I would be very surprised,' Loup drawled, 'if you were to discover his killer within these walls.'

'Who is dead?' asked Mistretta, setting the coffee down on a low table before pouring it.

'Our Henri Sabat,' said Loup.

'Murdered?' said Mistretta, a cloud falling over his eyes, 'How could Henri's luck run out just like that?'

'Everyone's luck runs out in the end,' said Loup.

'I am sorry to hear that Commissaire,' said Mistretta, 'he was a true gentleman.'

'And a good old-fashioned tipper eh Mistretta?' said Loup.

'Did you see him on Monday too, Monsieur Mistretta?' I said.

'Just to say hello and goodnight. He was happy when he left. I think he had done quite well for himself.'

'Did he leave on his own?'

'Not this time. He was usually alone. He would walk too,' growled Mistretta, 'he was a big, confident man.'

'Besides,' said Loup, 'people understand not to touch my regular customers. They know trouble will find them out.'

'Who did Sabat leave with on Monday night?'

'Some new friend of his,' said Mistretta, 'not the sort we usually get in here.'

'What sort is that?'

'He was a Corsican. You know, bullish at best and unpredictable at worst. I'm not the sort to walk on eggshells, but the look in that one's eye made me hesitate,' said Mistretta, 'He was missing part of his right ear, the bottom part where an earring might hang.'

'Did Sabat arrive with this gentleman?' I said.

'I couldn't say for certain,' said Mistretta.

'Did you meet this man Monsieur Loup?' I said.

'No. I don't believe I did. I went to bed early on Monday. Busy weekend you understand.'

'Indeed, I do,' I said, half closing my eyes as Loup's South American beans worked their magic, the thick, black liquid took me straight back to Cayenne. I struggled to return to the point of my visit. 'One final question.'

'Yes Commissaire?'

'It seems your man here knew me on sight before I introduced myself. I have been in the city barely three days and only just managed to meet the mayor.'

'Forgive me Commissaire Bassé, Bayeux is not such a big city,' Loup leered and immediately had me thinking of the sign hanging on the corner of the building, 'I have many interests, business interests that depend upon knowing what is happening, who is in town, that sort of thing.'

'If you hear anything concerning the fate of Henri Sabat through your interests in the city.' I paused, 'I would be grateful if you could let me know.'

'Of course, Commissaire, and I do hope that your next visit is simply for pleasure.' Loup licked his lips, 'I should enjoy being entertained by your mastery of the card deck.'

'Perhaps,' I said.

'I will send you an invitation sir, you may count on it.'

'Indeed,' I said and stood up to leave.

Mistretta held the door open for me, 'Until we meet again Monsieur.'

'Good evening Commissaire,' nodded Loup.

The sun had entirely vanished while I had been supping in the den of the wolf. The cold rose from the ground like a haunting. I stalked off into the darkened streets with an eye out for the eyes I knew must be watching me.

Was there a gambling man in the commissariat, sitting in Loup's pocket? Or perhaps he had eyes in the mayor's office? Perhaps the café? I told myself to calm down. There were fools enough in the donjon who could have let Loup know there was a new police inspector in the city.

Loup was a patron, a boss, he needed to appear to be in control of his business, and his interests. I shrugged. He was also a liar, of that I was absolutely certain. I would have to find more reliable witnesses. I had said nothing of the circumstances of Sabat's death, but murder had been readily assumed. That told me more than any fanciful tale of Corsican conspirators.

On the way back I passed by Jean-Luc Reynard's joinery shop. The lights were on in the office, so I knocked on the door.

'Stefan, come in, come in,' said my old friend, 'I'm just finishing up for the day. Do you want to come in for supper?'

'I do indeed,' I said, 'that would be wonderful.'

'What brings you this way?' Jean-Luc grabbed my hand and slapped me on the back, genuinely pleased to see me.

'Just work. I had to pay a visit to Monsieur Loup.'

'You going to put him in jail?' laughed Reynard.

'Should I?'

'That crook? Of course.' He threw his arms wide, 'He cheated poor old Jean so many times he ended up working for Loup on top of his regular work. Mortain lost hundreds of francs.' Reynard sighed, 'He had to pay it off but couldn't with the little he got from his father's shop, so he spent nights cheating for Loup.'

'What's your evidence?'

'Just what Jean told me. He'd come past here too some mornings, and I would give him some bread and coffee before he got to the shop.'

'Does Marie know?'

'I couldn't say, but with what Jean said he owed I'm sure Loup will let her know soon enough.' Jean-Luc grabbed me by the shoulder, 'Lock him up, Stefan.'

'I will one day,' I said, 'but I will do it the right way, so he never comes out again.'

'You will be doing all of Bayeux a favour. That wolf needs to be chased out of town for good.'

'So, what's for supper?' I had to change the subject.

'Stew. Always Amandine's stew on a Thursday.'

'Of course. I love stew,' I said.

'Come on then old friend, let's go,' he said.

Reynard still lived in the old family home attached to the workshops. After bolting the doors, I followed him past the stacks of dried, milled timber and drank in the scents of fresh-cut pine and the smoky, dusty presence of oak and walnut.

'You have a good stock in,' I said.

'Business is good Stefan,' he said, 'with all the new houses that are being commissioned, I am getting enquiries almost every day for doors, windows, shutters, and staircases. I have to turn work away or make them wait.'

'Where is it all coming from?'

'I know,' said Jean-Luc, 'things have been difficult for so long, but now France is turning the corner, and we are all feeling the benefit at last.'

He pulled open a door and a blast of warm air hit me. I had been here before many times as both man and boy, sharing a bowl of broth or some bread. It had always been a welcoming, friendly place and it seemed nothing had changed, except that time had passed. There was old Monsieur Jean-Pierre Reynard, Jean-Luc's father, in a chair close by the range, his hands curled in on themselves with arthritis, but still able to hold a pipe or a pencil.

'I look after the difficult jobs my boy hasn't learned yet,' he joked as we shook hands, 'not that there's much left for him to learn.'

Jean-Luc Reynard's mother Marie was a kind woman but for years I had been terrified of her second sight. It was as if she could read a boy's mind at a hundred paces, and I was concerned that she may have retained the ability.

'Stefan,' she said, 'it's good that you have come home. You were missed.'

'It is good to be back Madame,' I said, 'I do hope I can stay.'

'You must go where duty takes you,' she said, 'but we will thank God that you are here for now.'

'Mother,' said Jean-Luc, rolling his eyes, 'Stefan is the new Commissaire de Bayeux. He has come to catch all the villains who have followed the new money into town.'

'Well, there are plenty of them to keep you busy,' said Marie, 'you will be here for some time I fear.'

'He's met Loup already,' said Jean-Luc.

'They can have him on Devil's Island,' said Amandine, as she served stew into deep bowls, the aroma filled the room, 'surely you can get him a ticket on that boat Stefan?'

'Fast work,' said old Jean-Pierre.

'I take it you have had dealings with the man?' I said.

'He wanted to help the business,' said Jean-Luc, 'he's a man with fingers in everyone's soup bowl, or at least he tries to be.'

'What happened?'

'He wanted some joinery but tried to put more money through his account than we had ever seen before. He said it was how they did things back in Strasbourg. German accounting, he said.'

'Bank robber,' muttered Jean-Pierre.

'There was a rumour,' said Amandine, 'that he robbed a bank in Metz before he came to Bayeux.'

'You must have noticed his Alsace accent?' said Jean-Luc. I had and said so.

'But there are other rumours,' said Jean-Luc, 'that he was a refugee from the Alsace-Lorraine, that the authorities took his chateau and his lands.'

'The truth is often simpler than that,' I said.

'He's a crook,' said Marie.

'Just so madame,' I said.

'Supper is ready,' said Amandine.

And so, we ate.

Chapter Eleven.

Louis-Arsène Le Loup was sitting in his private salon with his right-hand man, Joe Mistretta, sipping his evening brandy and coming to terms with the latest changes at the Bayeux Commissariat, out of sight of the man himself.

'What do you think, boss?' said Mistretta, rubbing his chin.

'I don't know,' said Loup, frowning into the fireplace, 'Bassé has a good poker face.'

'Do you think he knows?'

'How could he?' Loup turned to face his man, 'He came here on a hunch. He doesn't have anything except perhaps and maybe.'

'What?'

'He might have a need to play,' muttered Loup.

'Cards?'

'Piquet,' said Loup, his forehead wrinkling in concentration, 'if I remember well enough, he was the one that taught Mortain how to play.'

'How to cheat, you mean, boss,' Mistretta's eyes narrowed.

'No, the cheating was all Mortain trying to bridge the gap between ability and what fools call luck. From what I heard out of Jean Mortain's mouth, this Bassé is an expert at the card table.' Loup took a sip of brandy and chased it down with a little iced water.

'What do we do?' said Mistretta.

'Reel him in. Nobody's perfect. Nobody's that good. We'll give him a taste and then, gradually, get him in debt.'

'Nice.'

'We could take a year or two over it. Play the long game.' Loup smacked his lips together, 'Send out an invitation, but make sure he gets it in person, and when he's at home.'

'Right Boss,' Mistretta nodded, brightening up.

'He needs to know we know things about him.'

'Like where he lives?'

Yes.'

'Where does he live?'

'No idea, have him followed, Mistretta.'

'What if he is an expert?'

'If he wins, he wins,' Loup shrugged, 'but he can't win forever. Just having him walk through the front door is a win for us.'

'When you write the invitation, I will send the boy out.'

'We will do it tomorrow Mistretta.'

'What about Nolet?'

'That shrimp? He knows that if he talks, he's a dead man. If he doesn't, he might get shipped out of the country.'

Mistretta shrugged his enormous shoulders. 'I don't trust him.'

'Then send him a reminder of our interest in him.' Loup clapped his hands. 'We have someone there who can pass on a message. Make it happen.'

'Why did he not put him in the river?' Mistretta shook his head.

'Who knows Mistretta?' sighed Loup, 'The man is an idiot, and we are fated to have to tidy up after him.'

'He'd be out to sea by now.'

'Like Mortain?' Loup's eyes flashed.

'That was different boss.' Mistretta studied the floor.

'I need all of this mess to go away. It's bad for business. My partners will be asking questions.'

'What do we do?'

'We will have to give the Inspector whatever he needs to keep him from getting any closer than Nolet.'

Loup closed his eyes and leaned back in his chair. The interview with Mistretta was over. Realising this, his man left the boss alone in the private salon. As he pushed open the door the sounds of early evening patrons met his ears. Whether it was a freezing winter night or a sweltering summer eve the club was always making money.

Two men were leaning on the window by the door waiting to come in. They were young, likely journeymen, salesmen, or functionaries. Mistretta opened the door and one of them immediately brandished an invitation.

'Gentlemen,' Mistretta boomed, 'good evening and welcome.'

He stepped aside to let them in.

'We have a no-weapons rule,' he said.

'Of course,' said the first man. He and his companion handed over their hunting knives and a small revolver.

'Thank you. I will hold these in my safe. You may collect them when you are ready to leave.'

The men shrugged, shook his hand, and went through into the club. When Mistretta turned back to the front door he saw that the two he had thrown out earlier had returned.

'I thought I told you two not to come back,' he growled.

'You did,' said one.

'But we ain't finished,' said the other.

'Oh, you are,' said the doorman, 'you're finished here, make no mistake.'

'I think there's something wrong with your hearing,' said the first man, the other reached into his coat and pulled out a revolver. He pointed it at Mistretta and advanced into the hallway.

'Now we want our money back,' said the gunman, 'the money this cheating house stole from us.'

'You lost that money on the card tables to other customers,' Mistretta kept his voice low, 'the house of Loup owes you nothing.'

'We don't want to make this difficult.' The gunman jabbed his pistol at the burly doorman.

'I'm sure you don't,' said Mistretta. He rushed the gunman, knocking over his accomplice at the same time. There was a shot, a scream. Mistretta took the gunman by the wrist and began smashing his hand against the wall. The gun flew out of his hand and Mistretta kicked it away. The man lashed out, but the big man had him pinned.

'Oh dear,' said Loup, emerging from his salon, a pistol in each hand, 'you appear to have shot your friend.'

The doorman landed a blow on his captive, knocking him out cold.

'Is he dead?' asked Loup.

'No, just a graze. What shall I do with them?' said Mistretta.

'Put them in the stables. When they wake up, see if they need a job.'

Mistretta threw his head back and laughed, 'Will do boss.' He took one man under each arm and dragged them out through the door and around the back of the building to the stable block.

'Hey Fabron,' he called for the groom, 'I got two idiots for the Hole.'

'Okay, Joe.'

Fabron pulled open a door to what used to be a piggery. The space inside was too low for a grown man to stand up straight and was host to rats, spiders, and the odd noisy drunk.

Mistretta dropped the two men on the cold flagstones and slammed the door closed. There were no windows and only a little light made it in around the ill-fitting door. Somewhere in the darkness, a curious rat squeaked once, then dashed away.

'Let them shout, they can stay there until the morning.' Mistretta grinned at the old groom.

Fabron nodded, picked up his broom, and got back to sweeping the yard. It was getting dark, and he couldn't see what he was doing, but he had to do something to keep warm. In a half-hour, his shift would be over, and he could go home and sit next to the fire and cook his supper and dream of summer.

He thought about the long days that were still such a way off, the fetes, and the food that was to come. Fasting for Easter made that festival seem to take forever to arrive.

'Hey!'

The shout startled him from his reverie.

'Is there anyone there? My friend has been shot. We need a doctor. Anyone?'

Fabron stopped his sweeping. He did not want to make any noise that might encourage Joe Mistretta's guests. He began to back away slowly, treading as softly as he could.

'Hey! Somebody help us. A madman has locked us up. We are prisoners here.'

Fabron tiptoed away.

'You! You with the broom. Let us out. We won't tell anyone.'

Fabron kept on going toward the warm glow of the tack room. A horse snorted and stamped its feet. A dog appeared in the tack room doorway, a long-legged rangy animal. Fabron clicked his fingers and the dog, a hunting hound, trotted across the courtyard to the bolted door where the two dissatisfied customers had been billeted. It sniffed all along the bottom of the door, reading the scents of those inside, growling all the while.

The dog barked once, then turned, and ran back into the tack room, tail spinning behind him.

'Good dog,' said Fabron, and he patted the hound on the head, 'you told them.'

'Told who?' said an old snow-haired man who was slowly polishing a saddle that shone like he had been polishing it his entire life.

'Boys in the Hole,' said Fabron.

'Right.'

'Two of them.'

'Right.'

'Don't sound happy.'

'Never do, eh?'

'You about to finish there, mon ami?'

'Yep.'

'Come on then, let's go.'

'Right.'

Fabron started putting out the lights. He and the old man left the tack room door open for the dog and crossed the darkened courtyard to the gate. The dog followed, then doubled back to the door to the Hole and cocked his leg on it. Fabron chuckled.

'That's what the yard dog thinks,' he said.

'Yep,' said the old man.

Fabron made sure the gate was secure on the inside then the two men ducked through a low doorway into the main building. Behind them, they could still hear the shouts of the two prisoners.

'The one who got shot sounds well enough to me,' said Fabron.

'Right,' said the old man.

'Gentlemen,' their patron, monsieur Loup, appeared at the end of the corridor, 'how are my horses?'

'All well sir,' said Fabron. The old man said nothing.

'And my saddle. Is it gleaming?'

'It is that,' said Fabron.

'Very happy to hear it,' said Loup, 'I will see you gentlemen tomorrow.'

Loup turned and opened a door into one of the saloons. It had begun to get a little noisy. Thursday nights were usually more trouble than other times for reasons Loup had yet to fathom. His ambition was to make money properly, through a range of legitimate businesses, but this establishment remained more profitable than any other on his books.

He saw straight away who was causing the commotion and decided to intervene immediately. He strode across the room to the table where the argument was taking place and struck his walking cane on the floor three times. The men were silenced. They turned to their host.

'We are a civilised establishment, my friends,' he told them, 'Are you exercised by discrepancies in your game or by something else?'

Four young men stared back at Loup. They were a handsome quartet with expensive beards on youthful faces.

'Our apologies,' said one, 'we were talking about work.'

'Monsieur Arnaud,' said Loup, 'please refrain from shop talk. You come here to escape all that drudgery, non?'

'Of course,' said Arnaud, 'we apologise, don't we Gibert?'

'Yes, of course,' nodded Gibert. 'We will refrain from advising these gentlemen on their investment and instead enlighten their purses with our expert card playing.'

'Wise decision,' said Loup, nodding to the two prospects Arnaud and Gibert were hoping to beat. He knew Bouteloup and Vidu would probably show these two upstarts how grown men played the game.

Loup left the room and made his way back to his private salon. The fire had been built up and the room was warm and bright.

His mood rose and he rubbed his hands together at the thought of playing cards with the new police inspector.

'I will host the commissaire in here,' he mused aloud, 'or perhaps upstairs in the gallery?'

He tapped his long white teeth with a polished fingernail while he savoured the thought.

There was a knock at the door.

'Enter,' called Loup, and a large round-bodied, round-faced man waddled through the doorway.

'Vignes,' declared Loup. 'How very good to see you. How has your luck been lately?'

'Can't complain,' said Vignes, 'but they might be grumbling at the Horseshoe in Caen.'

'Why might that be?'

'I schooled them rather well last weekend and was asked to take a little holiday,' chuckled Vignes.

'Excellent work my friend,' Loup licked his lips, 'and you will be pleased to know those talents of yours will be exercised again soon. This time right here.'

'Sounds good,' said Vignes, 'we have a new mark?'

'A new, and potentially useful mark. One we have to play in a more subtle way than Caen.' He felt his mouth water.

'Tell me more sir wolf,' said Vignes.

Chapter Twelve.

I called for the investigating magistrate in the morning. Judge Tanquerel visited the hut where Sabat's body had been discovered and was pleased I had a suspect locked up at the Commissariat.

'Good work Bassé,' said Tanquerel, 'and you are gathering the evidence now?'

'Indeed, sir, although I am not certain that Nolet carried out the final act of murder, I am absolutely certain that he is guilty of covering up the act,' I said, 'and that he knows full well who struck the fatal blow. Sabat was a golden goose for Nolet, who was fond of feathering his own nest, so the motive is unclear.'

'You may be right,' said Tanquerel, 'but I am not convinced of his innocence. A jury would send Nolet to the gallows, seeing his conniving nature and lust for money as damning enough.'

'Sabat was dispatched with some confidence I believe,' I said, 'which leads me to believe that whoever killed him had killed before. I have sent my deputy Ouimet to question the staff at the hotel.'

'I wish you luck of course,' said the Judge, 'but I will be inclined to indict the concierge on Monday morning. You know how it is?'

The Judge inclined his head in the direction of city hall.

'I do sir.'

'Will that be all Bassé?'

'Not quite,' I said, 'forgive me but I understand that you were the investigating magistrate called to look into the disappearance of my father and stepmother?'

'That is true? Have you read the dossier?' The Judge was unmoved, having, I suspect, foreseen this enquiry.

'Not yet,' I admitted.

'I have nothing to add, but do you have new information that might shed light?'

'No sir, I have nothing to add as yet,' I said.

'I am sorry of course Bassé. It was a peculiar situation and I do not envy that you must live with it. I wish you luck, Inspector.'

'Thank you.'

We shook hands and the interview was over. I had until the end of the weekend to find enough evidence to convict Nolet, which would not be difficult, or find the actual murderer. I was reasonably confident it would not be Mistretta's mysterious Corsican.

I left the Palais de Justice and made straight for the Hotel du Theatre. Constable Desnier was at the front desk with Nolet's understudy, the night manager Chevrolet.

'Bonjour gentlemen,' I said.

'Bonjour Commissaire,' said Chevrolet, 'I am busy today with people leaving. Our guests heard about the murder, and they don't like the police being here.'

'It will all be over soon enough,' I said. 'How is Ouimet getting on Desnier?'

'He is in the dining room sir,' said Desnier, 'and I believe he is having a spot of breakfast.'

'Thank you, gentlemen,' I said, then made my way through.

'Deputy Inspector Ouimet,' I extended my hand to the plump moon-faced gentleman enthusiastically scooping scrambled eggs into his broad mouth.

'That's me,' he said brightly, taking a napkin and wiping his fingers before shaking my hand, 'I think I know who you are sir. Have you had breakfast Inspector? The chef here makes marvellous eggs.'

'I will have a coffee, have you had any luck with the staff or guests?' I was straight to business.

'Not a lot to tell really,' said Ouimet, 'all of them are agog that Nolet is behind bars.'

'Why is that?' I said.

'They all agree he's a weasel who would shave the donkey to get his share but none of them see him as a killer,' said Ouimet. He paused to spoon in a further mouthful of egg. 'He has a hiding place in his office so he can disappear should a guest be disagreeable.'

'Really?'

'Yes, it's full of all manner of things. He is a magpie as well as a weasel.' Ouimet scraped the remains of the egg from his plate with a scrap of baguette. 'And all the staff say Sabat would have easily flattened Nolet. He was a big man so if he did kill him it was either an ambush or he had help.'

'You might be right, but until we can identify an accomplice Nolet is all we have,' I said. 'My difficulty is that for a man as venal as Nolet, Sabat was too much of a golden goose. Where is the motive?'

'Greed?' shrugged Ouimet.

'Perhaps,' I said, 'I paid a visit to Monsieur Loup last night.'

'Right, so Nolet, he was a gambler?'

'No, Sabat,' I said. 'Loup painted a very rosy picture of a social gambler making business connections, that sort of thing.'

'Too good to be true?' Ouimet dabbed at his chin.

'Exactly,' I sipped at my coffee, 'so I am having a difficult time believing anything I hear at the moment. The Judge seems to think we have it all wrapped up.'

'Tanquerel?' Ouimet raised his eyebrows.

'I just came from his office,' I said, 'and his mind is made up. Nolet gets charged on Monday and sent for trial.'

'I read the interview,' said Ouimet, 'and from what I have gleaned here I am certain there is a missing link. Yes, Nolet is likely responsible for the death of Sabat, but he doesn't strike me as a man to get his hands dirty.'

'Indeed,' I said, 'my thoughts exactly.'

'There are two people I have not been able to speak to yet,' said Ouimet.

'Who's that?'

'The housekeeper and a stable hand.'

'Madame Omer is the housekeeper.' I said.

'You know her Inspector?' Ouimet raised his eyebrows.

'I know of her through my own housekeeper. These women make up an important network in the city.' I said. 'See what you can find out and try not to make an enemy of her.'

'I won't scare her sir,' said Ouimet, 'I have a way with housekeepers.' He winked. Somehow, I was not surprised.

I drank down the rest of my coffee and peered at the grounds in the bottom of the cup. I thought I could see a row of pointed teeth. I shuddered.

'When you're finished here Ouimet I want you to organise a watch on Loups' place. I want to know who visits, day, and night.'

'Have you got authorization from the Judge for that.' said Ouimet, 'I asked once about six months ago and was refused.'

'For what reason?'

Ouimet shrugged, 'He didn't see it as necessary to the case I was working on at the time.'

'But you did?'

'I was looking into a robbery, an amount of money taken from a jeweller and all roads led to monsieur Loup. I don't believe anything gets stolen in Bayeux without that man's say so.'

'I see. Do you have evidence?'

'I have begun a dossier, but it's slim and circumstantial at best,' Ouimet sighed, 'He is an expert at covering his tracks. The worst part of it is that a week later Inspector Hautefort tendered his resignation.'

'Is that so, Ouimet? How would that be connected? Hautefort was already past retirement age.'

'I don't know. It's just a feeling I had.'

'It's not your fault that Hautefort chose that week to go.' I said, 'The first rule of police work is, don't take anything personally.'

'You're right there, sir.' Ouimet managed a half-smile.

'So, what did you do?'

'I put a watch on Loup's place anyway, but it didn't get me the result I wanted. I think he got tipped off.'

'You took a risk there, and now you are taking a further risk by telling me.'

'I know,' Ouimet shrugged, 'but Royer seems to think you can be trusted, so that's good enough for me.'

'To be clear, your advice would be to not speak to the judge, not to go through the proper channels?'

'Not yet, sir. Not without something Tanquerel can't argue against.'

'That I can understand.' I said, 'I want to put Loup away if he is as guilty as my instinct says he is, but not at any cost, and it has to be watertight and done properly.'

'I have just the man for the job sir,' said Ouimet.

'A constable?'

'No, no one anyone knows.'

'Perfect, thank you,' I said, 'but remember, I do not need to know anything about your arrangements and this conversation never took place. Do you understand me?'

'I do, sir.' Ouimet held my gaze, 'It'll not be a trouble to you, Inspector.'

'Thank you, I think we might just get along very well, you and me. I will leave you to your duties and arrange whatever you will. In the meantime, I must get back to my office. I need to talk to Nolet again. I am so certain he knows who the killer is. It sits like a stone in my belly.'

I decided to take a walk across the city from the Hotel du Theatre to the commissariat. The weather was freezing, with ice still coating the cobblestones, and the dry smokiness of the air, the chill that struck the back of my throat with every breath threw me back to childhood days, to the morning walk to school or the Sunday morning dash to the boulangerie before church.

I have a recurring dream where I am part of the circus troupe known as the Flying Tarantellis. I am a small boy in these dreams, and I am holding the hands of my mother while we swing backwards and forwards on a trapeze, over the straw-covered circus ring. I can hear the gasps of the crowd below us as we go higher and higher, closer, and closer to the canvas roof of the tent.

I catch my mother's eye and she smiles at me before letting go. I fall away from her as she flies through the air, spinning and spinning, faster and faster until she disappears through the roof of the big top, leaving a hole through which I can see stars gently twinkling.

And she is gone. And I remain with my legs wrapped around the trapeze. I let her go. I look back and see that my legs are chained to the swing, and I have come to a halt six feet above the straw. The trapeze begins to spin slowly, revealing the silent audience who simply sit and stare. Sometimes I see my father in their number, other times old school friends and members of the cathedral congregation. Sometimes I see myself.

Every time I have the dream, I wake up just as a lion enters the ring. Almost every time. Last time, the creature was a wolf.

I have the dream as often today as when I used to drink. I have had it since my mother left us. My father was plagued by dreams too. I hope that wherever he may be now, that he has found some peace from them.

When I arrived back at the commissariat, I had no time to dwell on personal things. Sergeant Leverrier was waiting for me on the front desk in a state of agitation.

'Sir,' he said, 'there is a lady in your office. I am so sorry, and there's another one in the better interview room.'

'What do they want?'

'The lady in your office said she was here to make a statement and that she would wait all day if she had to because she would only talk to you,' said Leverrier.

'Very good,' I said, 'who is she?'

'Widow of the dead man we found in the river.' He held his breath.

'Thank you Leverrier I have been expecting her. You did the right thing this time by letting her into my office,' I said, 'but you had better not make a habit of it. Send up the stenographer and a carafe of water please.'

'Yes sir,' said a visibly relieved Leverrier.

'Who is the other woman?'

'A reporter,' Leverrier winced, 'I've not seen her before, but her papers were in order.'

'I'll see the reporter first,' I said, 'name?'

'Madame Angèle Foucher, she is with Le Matin.'

'Very good sergeant.'

A ship without a captain tends to drift and end up in trouble. I could see this commissariat needed steering.

The better interview room was the one with the window and upholstered chairs. We used it for witnesses and general visitors. The tricolour hung on the wall opposite the door, apart from that there was no decoration.

I knocked at the doorway. Madame Foucher was standing with her back to me looking out of the window at the square. She was a dark figure surrounded by light.

'Madame,' I said.

She turned around and remained in silhouette so I could not make out her features.

'I do not have much time. How may I help you?'

'Inspector, how good of you to spare me a moment,' her voice was surprisingly light and youthful, and as my eyes adjusted, I realised she was indeed quite young, and remarkably pretty, with piercing blue eyes that glittered with acute intelligence, 'I have recently arrived in the city, as have you, and felt it only polite to make your acquaintance as soon as possible.'

'Thank you,' I said, she had me on my guard immediately, 'it has been a matter of days.'

'Inspector, because of our mutual situation I am of a mind that we could be of benefit to each other.'

'In what way Madame?'

'I want to make a mark, change things, make things better and I thought that perhaps you might be able to point me in the right direction from time to time. As for my part, people say things in restaurants and official buildings that they do not suspect someone like me to notice.'

'I see,' I said, 'so an agreement is what you seek?'

'It is.'

'Such a thing takes time and trust Madame.'

'Then let me endeavour to win that trust, Inspector.'

'You say you are new to Bayeux. Why this city?'

'Le Matin had an opening, I interviewed, and they made me an offer. I had no other offers, so I am here.'

'Where were you before?'

'Rouen. I was a court reporter, writing about what had already happened. I want to write about things that are happening now. I don't want to wait until it's all over.'

I saw a momentary flash of anxiety in her eyes as if she felt she'd said too much. It was replaced in an instant by the cool steel gaze of ambition.

'I appreciate you coming to see me, Madame Foucher. I have had friends in the press before and know how valuable you can be, but I do not believe I have anything for you at the moment.'

'What about the murder?' Madame Foucher crossed the room at a march and came up short half an arm's length from me. 'Do you have the killer?'

Her perfume was almost overpowering in the cold air. Lemon with a hint of something I recognized from my time in the tropics. What was it? She held my gaze.

'Madame,' I started.

'Actually, it's Mademoiselle Angèle Foucher,' she said.

'Very well, Mademoiselle, yes,' I said, 'I believe we have the perpetrator, but that the case is more complicated than it first appears. We are investigating further because I do not want to leave any room for doubt. We owe it to the deceased to make sure we have the full story.'

'And when you have the full story, Inspector?'

'I will be in touch,' I said, 'and of course, should you come across any information that might help in completing the picture?'

'Likewise, I shall also be in touch.' With that Mademoiselle Foucher offered her right hand. I shook it, then saluted out of habit and escorted her from the interview room.

*

At the bottom of the stairs to my office, I paused a moment and took a deep breath. Jean Mortain and I had not seen each other in almost a decade. We had last met in Bayeux before I sailed from Le Havre for South America. Jean had drunk too much cider and wine and had been ill. Marie Daufresne, his wife, and I were the last of the small party of well-wishers still standing.

I remember the night sky seeming particularly bright that evening. We watched and waited for shooting stars, holding hands.

'Why are you leaving us?' Marie asked.

113

'You know I can't stay,' I said, 'don't make me say it all again, please Marie.'

'I will miss you,' she had said then. Not 'we', but 'I'. I was Jean's sensible friend, the one who would always make sure he got home safely after a long night out.

We were not to blame for the way we felt, we could not help it. We were in love and had been ever since that first night at the circus, in the dark magic of our teenage years. My father had forbidden me from seeing Marie. She was the daughter of a paysan, no matter where her education or ambition might have taken her. My father always knew best and had better in mind, for me, and for the family.

'Our ancestors were Kings boy,' he would intone, 'we must not let their memory down.'

But now my father was gone, and so was Jean, and so were ten years of our lives. The stairs creaked as I climbed to my office. The air had become thick as molasses. As I rose, I could see the door was open and there was Marie sitting with her back to me. The stenographer bustled past me and suddenly the molasses dissolved, and I was swept into my office in a rush.

'Good morning Madame,' I said, wincing on the inside.

'Stefan?' she said.

'Marie,' I took her hand, and she stood up, 'I am so sorry.'

'I know,' said Marie, 'but it has happened, and we must get used to it.'

'In time, we will, I suppose,' I said.

'I am here to make my statement,' she said.

'I know,' I said, 'thank you. The coroner's report states accidental death by drowning.'

'Yes, but,'

'I know, I found it hard to reconcile too,' I said, 'Jacques? Are you ready?'

He nodded.

'Then Madame Marie Daufresne, with your permission, let us begin.' I said.

'Thank you, Inspector,' she said.

'I will declare my personal interest for the record. I was close friends with the deceased, but I had not seen him for a number of years,' I said, 'Madame, when did you last see Jean Mortain, your late husband?'

'Almost a month ago. The streets were lit up at midnight by a great full moon. There was frost everywhere and it was quite beautiful, even if it was terribly cold,' she smiled at the memory, 'Jean had been quiet in the shop all day, but he had been busy with his other job. He was working playing cards for someone, not gambling, just entertaining, not like before.'

'Was there a time when gambling had been a problem?' I said.

'Yes,' she dabbed at her eyes, 'you know what he was like. He started out by winning so much money then threw it all away again. He lost so much at Loup's place that they made him work for the club, finding new blood for the tables. That man always needed a flow of new idiots to take money from.'

'Did Jean know Paul Nolet?'

'Yes, I think they were friendly,' said Marie, 'at least in matters of business.'

'You must forgive my impertinence, Madame,' I said, 'but I must ask whether, at the time of his disappearance, were you having money problems?'

'Yes, we did,' she maintained steady eye contact.

'Did you talk about them?' I said.

'We did. His father was due to retire so we planned to sell the shop and move to my cousin's farm at Vaucelles.'

'Would that have solved the problem?'

'No,' said Marie, 'I had hoped so but as soon as I arrived home after the funeral a small boy, an urchin, delivered this note.'

'For the record,' I said, 'I have been handed an envelope of fine vellum. Inside is a folded piece of paper.' I took it out and read the invoice from Loup's club. 'That is a lot of money,' I said.

'I know,' she sighed, 'I have paid him the proceeds of the sale of the shop, after paying Baartram and we are leaving Bayeux in a month for Vaucelles.'

'And the balance?'

115

'I must work at Loups' place to pay the debt.' Now she was embarrassed.

'You will not live long enough to pay off this debt.' I said.

'I know.'

'Jacques, that is all for now, thank you,' I said, 'Madame will sign the statement at the front desk shortly.'

'Sir,' Constable Jacques picked up his notebook and, with a nod to Marie, he left the room. When he had gone, I crossed to Marie and took her hand.

'How are the children?' I asked.

'Sad, of course,' she said, 'and Jean's father is heartbroken.'

'I understand,' I said, 'if he had another shop to sell, the debt would still not be cleared.'

'What can I do?' her breath was ragged.

'I will talk with this man, this Loup,' I said, 'I met him yesterday. I think I can make him see reason.'

'Then you will be the magician of Bayeux,' said Marie, 'or the boar who defeated the wolf.'

'I cannot see you and your family rot in some backwater,' I said, 'it's not right. I wish I could have returned at some happier time.'

'It's not your fault,' she said.

'I know, but I will call on you tomorrow with some better news,' I said, 'I promise.'

I let go of her hand. Neither of us moved for a long moment as we stood close together. Too close.

'I must go,' she said at last, and so I saw her out to the steps of the commissariat.

'Until tomorrow,' I said.

'Until tomorrow.'

I watched her walk away across the square, my mind and heart racing. Out of the corner of my eye, I spotted the reporter sipping coffee at Guillaume's.

Chapter Thirteen.

I did my paperwork through lunch and then went home, to my new rooms in my old home, to rest and prepare for the evening's activity that I had in mind. In the jungles of Guyana, I met a man who had mastered the art of sleep. He could make his bed up a tree, on a branch like a leopard, and sleep soundly for any set period of time, two hours, three perhaps. I tried to learn his technique, but it never really worked for me. I drank far too much rum and coffee in the tropics.

I had left written instructions in an envelope for Ouimet with Royer. The intrigue had raised the sergeant's eyebrows, but sometimes I find it necessary to play cards close to one's chest.

My wicked grandpa did not simply teach me card tricks, and my father, though retired from show business, still developed illusions he hoped to sell on. I was a sponge, soaking up all the magician's tradecraft. At the top of the house remained a room full of partially constructed stage props, blueprints, and sketches for fantastic creations never built and then one or two finished and ready to dispatch but going nowhere. I had seen the half-constructed illusions in action before and witnessed the clunking mechanics of magic and illusion feeding an audience's innate need to believe in miracles.

Illusion, not sorcery. Knowing that what was happening on stage was built from wood, and mirrors, with skill and precision, was what audiences wanted. It was legal and safe, understandable, and above all it was human. Sorcery was illegal for good reason. Breaking natural laws and using unearthly means to make magic was far too dangerous unless you were a licensed alchemist working for a Royal House or government.

None of his illusion machines had been covered up and everything sat beneath a thin sheen of dust which floated into the air as I brushed past this museum to my father's career. I spent almost an hour carefully opening boxes, trying to keep the memories closed up inside while searching for the single thing I thought I needed.

On the way out I spotted a box with my name inked in the clear, tall handwriting of my father. Inside were letters and pictures, old journals, and books I had read as a boy. I picked it up and carried it down to my rooms. I would go through it at my leisure. I had to start somewhere.

As I came down the stairs, I heard a knock at the front door. I was curious to know who might expect me to be home to callers, so I put down my box and went to open up. On the step was a ragged, skinny boy with a hat pulled down over his ears. He held aloft a small white square envelope.

'Monsieur,' he said, waving his hand.

'Merci,' I said and took the envelope. He held out his hand and I pressed a sou into his palm.

'Merci monsieur,' he said, his fist closed tight about the coin, and he bolted across the courtyard and into the square as if the devil himself was at his heels. I looked up and down to see whether I was being observed, then closed the door.

The envelope was of the same quality as the one Marie had shown me earlier. I slit it open and pulled out a neatly written invitation to play cards, as promised.

'Let battle commence,' I muttered to myself.

I took my time getting ready. 'Ninety-per-cent preparation,' my father had said, and he was right. I checked myself in the mirrors in the hall and decided that I would do.

Loup's place was a reasonable distance from my house. I thought perhaps it would be wise to take a cab. I could collect my thoughts and not be all consumed with keeping warm. I stayed my hand on the doorknob, the thought had suddenly occurred to me that someone could be watching the front. My host would know I was on the move, so what? When I emerged onto the front step a cab was waiting in the street.

'Commissaire,' said the driver, tipping his cap, 'ready when you are sir.'

I had not ordered this service and bridled somewhat at Loup's hubris in his expectation that I would jump at his call. I thought about turning around and going back indoors. I could simply stay at home. I could take the cab somewhere else, or I could rise above my pride. I tossed the driver a Franc.

'Take your time, driver,' I said.

'Absolutely sir.'

Part of me was pleased Loup seemed in a hurry to make my acquaintance at the table. Now I was more than ever determined to make him regret it.

All lights were burning at Loup's place and there was a small queue at the door. As my cab arrived the yard gates opened, and we drove inside the mews courtyard. The cab halted and I was directed to dismount and head for a short staircase to a covered patio where a short white-haired man waited. He was dressed up like a footman from one of Napoleon's palaces and held a small silver tray in his hands upon which he balanced a demi-tasse of coffee.

'Commissaire,' nodded the old man. He waved me through a door and followed with the tray. I found myself in a snug with a very welcoming warm fire and a comfortable chair. 'The master is not quite ready for you sir, so please sit and make yourself comfortable.'

I thanked the old man and gave him a small tip. I settled in by the fire and warmed up quickly. I liked the heat. Always had. Before coming out for the evening I had banked up the range at home in the hope it would keep me warm on my return.

The flames flickered in the grate. There was nothing else in the room to amuse me, so I sat and stared into the fire, watching the flames change colour as sap burst forth from one log and bark crackled with sparks on another. The effect was pleasantly soporific, and I found myself relaxing into a light snooze.

Eventually, the old man returned and tapped me on my shoulder. I climbed slowly to my feet and then followed him through another door and along a narrow corridor before we emerged into the entrance hall. It was empty and the queue had vanished. The door to Loup's private salon was open.

'Le Commissaire,' announced the footman, then stood aside to let me in.

119

'Bonsoir mon ami,' said Loup, his wide smile beaming at me. He offered his hand, and I shook it.

'Monsieur Loup,' I said.

'I do apologise for the charades, but I didn't want you to have to mix with my other clientele,' said Loup. 'I did not think you would see how highly I esteem this visit had I let you mix with a less, how can I put it, a less professional milieu.'

'Thank you,' I said, 'am I the first to arrive?'

'One gentleman is here already, let me introduce you to Monsieur Leopold Vignes,' said Loup. Vignes stood up to greet me. He was a veritable mountain of a man. 'He has an appetite, don't you Vignes, for all the good things in life, including card games.'

'Bonjour Monsieur,' I said, offering a hand.

'Bonjour,' said Vignes as he caught my hand in a giant fleshy paw.

'Inspector Bassé,' said Loup, 'with your name, I have met my match.'

'How so?'

'Bassé is the Old French for sanglier or wild boar. The wolf and the boar, the two beasts that will savage Vignes' purse and eat all his gold,' laughed Loup.

'You will get drunk on your own schooling Loup,' said Vignes, 'then I will bankrupt you.'

'Watch him, Inspector,' said Loup, still grinning, 'Vignes is extraordinarily competitive.'

'Someone once said that the card table is the ultimate battlefield for soldiers of fortune,' said Vignes.

'No one who ever went to war I'll wager,' laughed Loup, 'but the lady Fortune is my mistress and she and I will be winning on the battlefield tonight.'

'Who else will be joining us?' I said.

'Another professional gentleman,' said Loup, 'Doctor Vallet.'

'He can patch up your wounds, Loup,' said Vignes, 'once I've done with you.'

'Quite so Leo,' said Loup, 'quite so.'

'Doctor Vallet,' announced the footman.

A ravenous leer split Loup's head in two. 'Welcome Doctor, you know Vignes of course and let me introduce you to Bayeux's newest resident and police inspector, Commissaire Bassé.'

I saw the doctor blanche, but he recovered quickly, snatching up my hand and pumping my arm in a vigorous show of friendliness.

'Bonsoir Commissaire,' he said.

'So tonight, I am very excited,' exclaimed Loup, 'for now we have the good doctor, the medicine man at the table, the winemaker, who helps the medicine go down, and the policeman, who looks after all the rules the church do not care for, all here in my private salon.'

'If you burst, I'll not sew you up, Loup,' said Vallet.

'I will be fine,' said Loup, 'let us play. Cut for the dealer?'

'New cards first,' said Vignes, making himself comfortable at the table.

I took a seat to the right of Vignes and the doctor sat to my right. The wolf would be facing me, the boar. He had the teeth, but I had the tusks. In nature, for a wolf, a wild boar was a very dangerous proposition, better to be avoided.

Loup opened a new deck of cards. It was a fine print that I recognized as Parisian. It had its peculiarities but was renowned for its consistency. It would be impossible for a novice to read, and difficult for me.

'Aces?' I said.

'Low,' said Vignes.

'Low it is,' said Vallet.

Vignes won the cut took a second deck and shuffled the two together. At the same time, the footman arrived with glasses and bottles of calvados and whisky and a carafe of water for me.

'I admire your sobriety, Bassé,' said Loup. 'Perhaps one day you will be a Judge? Maybe one as successful as our Tanquerel?'

'Perhaps,' I said, 'but I am happy as I am for now. I am more active than a Judge needs to be.'

Loup laughed, Vallet scowled, and Vignes shrugged.

'I deal to my left,' said Vallet.

'Of course,' said Loup, 'let us begin.'

I watched and counted through the first hand, not expecting much more than a chance to read the three men. Piquet is a demanding game and requires discipline and patience, more so than chess. Those who dismiss it as just cards, or the refuge of villains have no idea of the complexities involved.

The doctor lacked patience and became fidgety when the game seemed to stall, biting at his lip. I lengthened my time contemplating my move and watched as his nerves suffered. Bad news for Vallet so early in the evening. He took on more calvados the more I delayed.

I wondered whether Vignes had spotted this tell also. He had the air of a bored grazing animal, chewing over every turn of a card, eyes half closed while taking regular, but tiny sips of his whiskey.

Loup simply grinned like a cadaver, his face fixed in a peculiar rictus, but I was certain I could see changes in the light in his eyes.

I sat upon my plinth as usual, the Stefan Statue, Mortain would call me. It worked for me.

We played in silence for the most part, except for the functions of the game. This was not a sociable evening, so far this was straightforward competition. I decided to open things up somewhat.

'Did you play Monsieur Sabat, Doctor Vallet?' I said.

'I beat him last week,' said Vallet.

'He woke you up at your hotel that night, did he not?'

'Yes,' said Vallet, 'How did you know that?'

'It is my job to know things, sir,' I said.

'Of course, I forget.'

'Can you confirm what time it was that you were disturbed?'

'No, but I can confirm that it was loud.' Vallet frowned, disapproving of the inquisition.

'What was?' I narrowed my eyes.

'When he was stabbed. He made a lot of noise. I had to complain.' Said Vallet.

'So thoughtless,' ginned Loup, 'not like dear old Sabat at all.'

'He was funny,' said Vignes, 'I liked him. He made losing money fun. Not like the doctor here. He takes it all too seriously.'

'Life is a serious business, Vignes,' said Vallet, 'and yours will be over soon if you don't start taking things seriously.'

'Well, I am serious in my work,' said Vignes, 'but this is not work, and my glass happens to be empty,' he added, reaching for the whiskey.

'Sabat was a good customer,' said Loup, 'so I am sad that he has gone. We all enjoyed his company and so, I propose a toast to Henri Sabat.'

We raised our glasses.

'And to Jean Mortain,' I said, 'a former employee of this house.'

'It has been an unusual and difficult week,' said Loup, hiding his teeth for a moment. 'This is not a normal state of affairs.'

'I should hope not,' I said.

'No doubt I would run out of customers and workers very quickly if it were usual,' said Loup. 'Of course, I know you knew Mortain as a friend Inspector, and you may find you will agree with me when I say he was not a model employee.'

'How so?'

'He preferred the bottle to all other vices. He played cards well, with some skill, but he would drink too much, no matter what,' said Loup. 'We sent flowers of course, but I fear his end was a predictable one.'

'What do you mean?'

'At this time of year, if you fall in the river drunk you will not last long.' Loup lost his jollity.

'I am not certain that Mortain drowned,' I said.

'What does your physician say?' said Vallet.

'He was too far along and had spent too much time on the riverbed for a definite answer,' I said, 'but there were signs that he had been tied before he went in the river. I saw the body before he was buried, and the marks were discernible.'

'Why am I not surprised,' said Loup, 'I doubt I was alone in being owed a small fortune by the man.'

'Who else did he owe money to?'

'Small fry, rough stuff from what I gather,' said Loup, 'just the sort to lose patience over a paltry sum, but that's enough work for now, monsieur policeman. Let us play some more cards.'

Chapter Fourteen.

If I had unsettled Loup, he did not show it. A clear professional, he gave little away. I spent time watching and learning as the stakes gradually rose. No one was winning or losing any more than anyone else, but I got the sense that this was simply the warmup.

'I received my second big interest payment from that new man, the Notaire on the Rue Des Bouchers,' said Vallet.

'What did you do with it?' said Vignes.

'I paid it directly back to the Notaire as a reinvestment,' said Vallet.

'With the same man?' asked Vignes.

'Of course,' said Vallet, 'I'd be a fool not to at those rates.'

'You would be better off bringing that money to this table,' grinned Loup, 'mark my words, Doctor.'

'It's not too late if you want in,' said Vallet, 'I am certain my good name and standing with the Notaire would enable you to join the investment cartel.'

'I said at the time that it was too good to be true, Vallet,' said Loup, 'but he has paid a year's rent in advance on his offices, so I will take that as my reliable dividend.'

'You are simply becoming more cautious in your old age, Loup,' said Vallet, 'just look at the paltry stakes we are playing for tonight.'

'Now, now Doctor,' said Loup, 'you might make a fortune selling chalk pills and smelling salts to dust dry dowagers but our guest of honour here is a simple public servant and I dare not embarrass him.'

'I'm sorry, I did not realise this was not a serious endeavour this evening. Should I retire now?' said Vallet.

I held up my hand.

'Gentlemen, Doctor,' I said, 'please do not hold back on my behalf. I assure you that my time in French Guyana amongst the gold prospectors was spent most profitably.'

'Happy to hear it,' said Loup, his smile so broad I thought it might reach right around his head, 'so let us not be shy then Doctor. I will start at twenty-five Francs.'

'Very well,' Vallet smirked, 'I see your twenty-five and raise by another twenty-five.'

Vignes matched Vallet and Loup and then all eyes were on me.

'Inspector?' purred Loup.

'Fifty francs,' I put them in the centre of the table with the rest, 'and another fifty.'

The dynamic around the table changed immediately. Expressions hardened, the game had been taken up a notch. Their individual tells might be reined in, but they would still be there, and I had learned some of the giveaways.

I counted the cards throughout the game. I could recognize several now from their prints and had a good idea of how this hand was going. It would be a win for Vignes. When it happened, I saw an unmistakable look of disgust pass across the doctor's face. Loup saw it too and could not suppress a laugh.

'We need a toast to your first big win of the evening, Vignes,' he said, 'Mistretta.'

'Yes sir,' Mistretta emerged from an alcove by the door. I wondered how long he had been there.

'Where is Isabelle?'

'In the kitchen sir.'

'Get her scrubbed up,' he said, 'I need a friendly face to keep my calvados glass filled up.'

'Right away sir.'

'You won't distract me with your pretty girls Loup,' said Vignes, 'I will still beat you whatever tricks you try.'

'I do not begin to understand what you mean,' said Loup, 'Isabelle simply has the steadiest calvados pouring hand I have ever seen.'

Vignes looked at me and winked.

'He doesn't keep this girl around for her steady hand,' he said, 'you will see what I mean.'

'That is quite enough of that,' said Loup, 'now let me win some of that money back. Inspector?'

'Yes?'

'Your deal.'

'Of course,' I shuffled the decks together and dealt the cards around the table. I had a good hand, as did Vallet. He pushed the stakes higher than before while I remained quietly matching every raise.

I narrowly beat the doctor. It was close, but I was prepared to lose as I had something in reserve. Now I could easily last until dawn if I had to. Vallet tried as hard as he could but that look of disgust forced its way through his card player's mask.

'So, Doctor, now our policeman can place a proper gentleman's bet,' said Loup, 'what do you say?'

'I would agree,' said Vallet, 'if he has the stomach and, as much as I hate to see our public servants impoverished, I am certain that he will receive far greater rewards in heaven.'

'And a small blow against the burden of the state,' said Vignes.

'True,' said Loup, 'we pay our taxes so good men get their wages. The Inspector will never go hungry in my city.'

'I am not finished eating yet, Loup,' I said.

'Less parlay more cards,' said Vignes.

'Where is that wench,' growled Loup. He then recovered himself as a tall, dark-haired woman entered the room.

'My favourite server is here at last,' said Loup.

She leaned over at the table to pour Loup's drink, sidestepping in time to keep a roving hand out of reach. Vignes looked her up and down, appraising her as one might a horse at market. Only Vallet appeared unmoved.

When she stood up, I caught her eye. Loup might call her Isabelle, but I knew her as Marie Daufresne. I could feel my host's dead gaze, but I knew how to hold my nerve and had played for high stakes before. Marie was working off Jean's debt, but she had no chance if she remained in the kitchen.

'Isabelle, this is not a wake for lost friends. We are not at a funeral. This is a celebration. Go and get changed into that red dress I bought for you.' Loup did not speak directly to Marie but kept his eyes on me the entire time. I shuffled the cards, unmoved by the drama Loup had tried to play. I had, after all, been raised in the theatre tradition. Isabelle-Marie left the room in a hurry, but not without dignity.

'You are in for a treat Vignes,' said Loup, 'I saw Isabelle in her red dress earlier this evening, and it enhances everything you like best in a woman.'

'Really?' said Vignes.

'Absolutely. She will keep your mind off the game just enough for me to beat you,' said Loup, 'not that I wouldn't beat you anyway.'

'Why don't you call for a boy for Vallet,' said Vignes, 'and a criminal for the Inspector.'

'A boy. What a good idea, Mistretta?'

'Yes sir?'

'The new croupier?'

'Maxim?'

'He can serve Vallet.'

'Right away sir.'

'And as for the Inspector, well I don't know of any criminals at all,' grinned Loup, 'I fancy there will be little here to entertain the Inspector and if Vallet is correct, we need not worry too long before the money counts him out.'

'I would be sorry to disappoint,' I said, 'I have often been underestimated by men in your position, however, I admit I am not here for the company, but for the cards.'

'Shame,' said Loup, 'I was trying to like you.'

'No need,' I said, 'now shall we play?'

I dealt the cards and almost immediately, and without even inspecting his hand, Loup put in a thousand francs. Each of us followed suit. Loup then raised the stake by another thousand. Vignes followed, a little reluctantly I thought. I waited, making Vallet sweat before folding. I was out this time around. Vallet raised again, Loup followed, and Vignes held on for the sake of dignity.

The doctor then hesitated, debating the balance between winning and losing. Eventually, he made his decision and asked for a card. Loup followed as did Vignes. The table was silent. No one was breathing. Vallet raised another five, Loup matched, and Vignes had to keep pace. Vallet took his time again. I could see a tiny flicker in his eyes, the greedy little demon that dragged a loser back to the tables again and again. I knew, and he almost knew, his hand was unbeatable.

The good Doctor Vallet pushed the stakes up another thousand.

'I am out,' said Loup, 'Vignes?'

Vallet had won.

'Well done sir,' said Loup, 'I think, however, that you should give us a chance to win a little back.'

'Certainly, Loup,' said Vallet, 'I am more than happy to empty your safe tonight.'

The young croupier arrived and stood to attention between me and Vallet and did not move a muscle. The doctor pretended not to notice him but was clearly pleased with the young man's presence.

I kept the pack and dealt again. Vallet won well again and became somewhat tipsy on his success. Loup insisted we play again to restore his fortune in a sporting manner. I retained my place as the dealer at the insistence of Vallet, 'If you can't trust the gendarmerie then where will it all end?'

I had begun the shuffle when Isabelle-Marie returned to serve drinks at the table opposite me. The red dress was a light-weight confection more suited to the more sordid theatres in the back streets of Paris. She avoided eye contact with anyone at the table as she refilled their glasses.

'There, Vignes,' grinned Loup, 'much better, much more becoming attire for a serving girl, yes?'

'I will not be distracted Loup, not when I have so much to win back,' he said, 'but she does look the piece.'

'I see you are unmoved Doctor Vallet, but I feel you must appreciate the stature of the fine young gentleman at your side?' Loup's leer was almost deranged when he turned to me, 'And Commissaire, I believe our serving girl is known to you, am I right?'

'The lady is known to me,' I said.

'Hardly a lady,' sneered Vallet, 'wearing whatever it is she is almost wearing.'

'Now come on Doctor,' said Loup, 'you must understand that our policeman friend does not mix in the heady circles you might be accustomed to?' Loup fixed his gaze on me, 'I don't doubt that the Inspector holds this particular woman in a higher esteem than you might expect.'

'I have no doubt he knows her on a professional basis,' said the doctor, 'now can we shut up and play cards, please? I am tired of your tittle-tattle sir, but not of taking your money.'

'Deal Commissaire,' said Loup, then clicked his fingers. Isabelle-Marie jumped to his side and poured calvados into his glass.

'Don't move a muscle serving girl,' he said, and put a hand squarely on her backside. 'She has a fine rump this filly Vignes, you should feel for yourself.'

'I will inspect the flesh later when I have finished counting your money,' said Vignes.

'It will cost you, Vignes,' said Loup.

'I know,' said Vignes, then to me. 'Whatever happens, you know Loup will be making money somewhere.'

We took up our cards. Loup started with a thousand francs at the table again and was immediately followed by Vignes. I made a show of thinking, then followed suit before Vallet could say anything. The doctor matched and doubled the stake.

I would not be able to keep up with the doctor if he kept up his quest for glory. I knew what he held in his hand was not the best selection of cards at the table, but he could win by betting me out of the game. I felt a bead of sweat develop on my forehead. The next move belonged to our host. No doubt he would match Vallet, perhaps even raise, suspecting the doctor may be playing on his winning streak.

Loup caught my eye and started to lift the hem of Marie's dress. She remained motionless as his hand revealed more of her legs.

'You will not put me off that way,' said Vignes.

Loup dropped his hand.

'You want her afterwards Vignes, she's yours,' said Loup, 'win or lose, I don't care.'

I felt sweat run slowly past my ear. Vignes had a little spittle forming at the corner of his mouth. I looked at my cards again and waited. Sure enough, Loup raised the stakes again. Vignes sighed and put his money on the table. I pushed forward all my remaining money, raising the stakes again. Loup raised his eyebrows but then Vallet took out a chequebook. To match his bet, I would need to sell my house. Loup rose to the occasion, but Vignes folded.

'I must look over the merchandise,' he said and waved Isabelle-Marie over and pulled her onto his lap.

'Inspector,' said Loup, 'what will you do?'

'I am in if only I can get a line of credit from the house,' I said, 'would that be possible, monsieur?'

I was certain that Loup's grin could not get any wider without causing him some medical distress. I was grateful we had a doctor at the table.

'Of course, Commissaire Bassé,' he said, 'as much as you like. I know I will be able to rely on a good public servant to uphold his obligations.'

'Quite so,' I said, 'thank you.'

It was all Loup could do to stop himself from rubbing his hands together. I wrote a promissory note on a sheet of notepaper produced at my shoulder by Mistretta. I thought for a moment. I could go too far, and Vallet might get cold feet. I needed Loup to see me in debt for more than just a moment. I matched all bets but raised by another two thousand. Before the ink had time to dry the doctor was scribbling out another cheque.

Loup waved to Mistretta who delivered more banknotes to his boss on a silver tray. Vignes, who had been more interested in the woman on his lap up until then suddenly returned his attention to the game. Vallet had pushed the stakes higher still.

This had become the most expensive game I had ever been a party to. I had played in Paris, Rouen, Cayenne, and New York where there were some very serious players. I had seen others win and lose big stakes, but I had always been more cautious, building up a solid nest egg, most of which now sat in the middle of the gaming table in front of me.

I knew, of course, that Loup had only stayed in the game because he needed me to owe him money. If we both lost to Vallet, Loup would win himself a police inspector. Loup could not beat either of us with the cards he had. I would also end my days in the gendarmerie barracks. If I beat Vallet then Loup would get all his money back and a happy policeman. Either way, it was a win for the house of Loup.

The wolf matched Vallet's reckless bid, leaving me some room to manoeuvre. I appreciated it and pushed Vallet another few thousand. The doctor was soon writing again. I was worried. Had I misread the cards? Was Vallet's hand better than I thought? I studied my cards. The hand was strong. Few combinations could beat it.

Loup folded. It was up to me to take or leave the bet. I wrote another note and matched Vallet. He raised his eyebrows.

'That is a lot of money there, monsieur gendarme,' said Vallet, 'you could do a lot of good with that, but I fear I could do more.'

'I doubt it,' I said, 'are you going to raise me again?'

'And have you mortgaged for life to our host?' said Vallet, 'There is nothing I would like to see more. I will raise you five thousand.'

Marie gasped, Loup snickered, and Vignes burped.

'I'll do it,' I said, 'but I don't wish to bankrupt you, sir.'

We sat staring across the table at each other as we laid cheque upon cheque. At last, Vallet appeared to have grown suddenly very tired.

'I will see you,' he said.

I put my cards down one by one and slowly the colour drained from the doctor's face.

Chapter Fifteen.

'I admit it,' said Loup, 'I underestimated you Inspector Bassé, we all did.'

'Everyone always underestimates the boar,' I said, 'that's how you lost to me, monsieur Loup.'

'I will beat you next time,' he said.

'If I let you,' I said, 'now here are your promissory notes, and here is a little bit of interest.'

'You are too kind,' Loup was still smiling, 'and what will you do with the rest? Will you find a comfortable mayoral role somewhere?'

'What? No,' I said, 'the rest of this money is all yours too.'

'Pardon?'

'It comes to something over what Jean Mortain owed you after you took his family business.'

'What? I don't understand?'

I saw Loup's self-control slip for just a second, a glimmer, a peek behind the curtains, a look into the wildness that I suspected lay hidden. There was a monster inside this gentleman, contained, controlled, willed into this human straitjacket. How far could I, should I provoke him?

'It's simple. I have settled my friend's debt and that of his widow.' I said.

'Never underestimate the boar,' chuckled Loup, 'but the wolf will have a turn yet my friend.'

'Here,' I showed him the invoice he sent to Marie for debts owed.

Loup took it and crossed it through signing and dating it at the foot of the page.

'It is done,' he said, 'Vignes, get your hands off that lady. I will have to find you another.'

Marie jumped up from Vignes' lap and pulled her red dress tight around herself.

'And it was all done so well,' said Loup, 'Jean told us you were a master of the game and I have to conclude that he was absolutely right. I have never seen a better cheat.'

'What?' cried Vallet, who had, until then, been in a deep sulk, 'I knew it. Give me back my money.'

'Shut up Doctor,' snapped Loup, 'Bassé, you and I should join forces. With your skills, we could tour the houses of Europe and clean them all out together. We could take Vignes, and you could send money back to your widow.'

'No Loup,' I said, 'I am taking Marie home now.'

'I have changed my mind,' said Loup, 'you didn't win fairly so the debt stands, and the win does not.'

'This was a private game and I won fairly. I imagine that is what you are upset about. I played by the rules and still beat you,' I crossed the room to stand face to face. I could feel his breath on my skin. I searched his eyes for that flicker, that tell-tale of blood rushing, of sinews readying themselves. 'I know it's difficult for you, but you and I have to come to an understanding.'

'No Bassé.' He was struggling to speak; his tongue was suddenly too big for his mouth. 'This is my city.'

'Loup.'

'What?'

'I have finished with being polite.'

I brought my right fist in fast and hard onto his nose, followed by a swift left, another right into an eye then I ducked around, looking for his henchman Mistretta. Another left on the nose sent blood all over the table, all over the huge pile of cash. A knee in the stomach and a right fist to the head and he was down on all fours.

I took Marie by the arm and pulled her out of reach of Vignes, who looked stunned. Vallet had his head buried deep in his arms and was oblivious. The croupier was nowhere to be seen. Mistretta appeared in the doorway and took in the scene with one glance. I reached into my coat and threw a smoke bomb over my shoulder. There was a crackle as a green cloud erupted and smoke began to fill the room.

I pushed Marie over to a window. Together we pulled it open and released the shutters. I helped her out into the street before I jumped down after. I threw a couple more bombs through the window then we ran up the road toward town where I had a cab waiting. We took off for the city centre. No one followed.

I began counting. One, two, three, four, five, six, breathe.

'What did you do all that for Stefan?' asked Marie.

'I think I made an enemy,' I said as I measured my breath.

'Of Loup, yes, I believe you did,' said Marie, 'but, you know, I had a plan. He wasn't going to get away with what he did to Jean.'

'But whatever happens now you owe that man absolutely nothing.' I said, 'If he wants more, he will be coming to see me.'

'I was going to kill him, Stefan.'

'What?' Three, four, five, six, breathe.

'I was going to poison him. I worked in the kitchens. It would have been easy, but now I won't get the chance.'

I could see in her eyes that Marie meant what she said. I was shocked but decided these were the words of a grieving widow and surely not those of a murderess.

'A man like Loup doesn't deserve an easy death, poisoned in his sleep. He needs to suffer. You would end up in prison, never seeing your children again.'

'No one would have known it was me, Stefan.'

Her jaw was set. I could see that she desperately wanted some form of justice. One she was certain that neither I nor the entire commissariat could deliver.

'I would have known Marie,' I said, 'You would've made a mistake. Murder isn't as easy as you think.'

'I daresay you're right. I expect you've met hundreds of murderers and you've probably killed men too.'

'What?'

'Killed someone,' she said.

'I might have done it in the line of duty, in self-defence, but never premeditated.'

'You look like you've thrown a good few punches in the ten years you've been away too. You never used to.'

'Sometimes it is the only way to get through, the only language they understand.'

'You are not the Stefan I remember,' she said, 'when that man left for Paris he was very by the book.'

'Reasonable force is in the book,' I said, 'I have had more practical experience since then, that's all.'

Four, five, six.

'Do not misunderstand. I am grateful I suppose,' she said, 'that Vignes is disgusting. He has terrible breath, and his hands are wet like he just returned from the bathroom,' she shuddered at the memory, 'so where are we going?'

'I am taking you home,' I said, 'and tomorrow you must find a different job.'

'I will never go back to Loup's. He can keep the old rags I wore in his kitchens.'

'Your business with that place is ended, and if anyone comes to see you, let me know. I will deal with Loup.'

'Can you?'

'What do you mean Marie?'

'I won't sleep properly until that man is in his grave.'

'He won't trouble you anymore, I promise.' I said, 'And I am certain he will be locked up for good one day, in a cold stone prison, where he belongs.'

'I hope you are right Stefan.'

The driver knocked on the roof of the cab.

'Here we are,' I said. I handed Marie down and walked her to the door of the house.

'You know I can't stay here,' she said, 'and I think it's for the best.'

'Marie?'

'Yes Stefan?'

'I cannot see you and the children move out to Vaucelles. You deserve better, and Elena and Guillaume will never get the education they deserve out in that swamp.'

'We have no choice, thanks to Loup.'

'Not yet but I have hope. I have a plan.'

'Thank you, now let me go, it's freezing out here.'

I watched her go inside and then, as I got back into the cab, I saw something dark skitter away in the shadows, back the way we had come.

'Commissariat,' I called out to the driver, and off we went.

I cleaned myself up in the building's washroom. My hands were bloodied, and I had torn my coat on the window catch as I left Loup's club. Afterwards, I went up to my office and slept on my chaise for a few hours until the day shift arrived.

I was awoken by Royer coming in with a black coffee and a pain au chocolat.

'Your brother, the boulangère, is going to make me fat,' I complained.

'I can't blame my brother for your waistline, sir,' said Royer, 'but I can stop bringing them in if you wish?'

'No, no Royer, I am still happy to receive them.'

'They are the best in town.'

'Of course,' I said, 'now what is the news in town this morning?'

'Not much. Reports of smoke and sorcery at a club on the edge of the city,' Royer's eyes narrowed, 'bit of a risky business.'

'No sorcery, just a simple smoke bomb. Where is Ouimet?'

'He is here sir.'

'Ah, good morning Ouimet. Anything interesting come up at the hotel?'

'A stable hand has gone missing. He was a favourite of Sabat's, would run errands and do special jobs for him.'

'What sort of special jobs?'

'He would attend to the monsieur's toilet,' said Ouimet.

'Who told you that?'

'The housekeeper, Madame Omer.'

'And?'

'He has been missing since last night, along with an amount of money from the safe. The madame could not say how much, or when it was taken, but that it belonged to Sabat she is certain.'

'I'm sure she is Ouimet, but that does not make it true.'

'I have men out looking for him. He has not been seen at the railway station and none of the cab drivers has seen him.'

'Gone to earth,' I rubbed my forehead with my thumb, 'thank you, Ouimet.'

137

'I am thinking he had the means and the motivation, and now we have Nolet under lock and key, he saw his chance, his moment to go.'

'Name?'

'Giancarlo Loparelli.'

'An Italian?'

'It's a hotel sir,' said Royer.

'Time we spoke to Nolet again Sergeant,' I said.

'On my way sir.'

'Bring him up here.'

'Yes sir.'

'Inspector,' said Ouimet, 'what happened at Loup's last night?'

'What? Did I not ask you to put a watch on the place?'

'I did sir, but I fear he may have been seeing things?'

'It's alright. I paid the criminal classes a visit. I schooled them all at the card table awhile and threw a few smoke bombs before liberating an old friend from a difficult position.'

'I see,' said Ouimet.

'Loup was intoxicated by the prospect of putting a police inspector in his debt. I suspect he already owns more than one of the men who work here.'

'I don't play cards Inspector,' said Ouimet, 'never really enjoyed belote, and it's all they would play where I grew up.'

'Good for you,' I said, and I meant it, 'the cards are easy to stack against a person. I was lucky last night, but Loup will never let me get that lucky again at his club, not without his say-so.'

'You're not going back there are you?'

'He is a criminal,' I said, 'so I expect our paths will cross again before we put him in prison.'

'Did he have something to do with Sabat?'

'Definitely Ouimet. That particular winter wolf knows more than he will ever tell me.'

'My watchman told me about the disturbance last night and that you were followed by a creature.'

'A wolf?'

'A werewolf.'

'Well, it's no secret where I or my companion live,' I yawned, but couldn't conceal my smile. I'd broken through Loup's resolve, made him show his nature, 'I was hoping Loup might give up Nolet. He could have done.'

'Perhaps he needs to keep his distance?'

'No Ouimet,' I rubbed my eyes, 'Loup is too greedy for that. He calls himself a man of business. He is a landlord. He likes money, the control of money, and the control of people. Last night I delivered chaos and turned his ideas about money on their head.'

'I was going to say, if you won so much, where is it?'

'I paid a debt, Didier.' I suddenly felt exhausted.

'A debt?'

'In full,' I yawned, 'but in Loup's world that's not how it works. In Loup's world, he owns you until the debt is paid, and the trick is, it never is.'

'Not your debt?'

'No, that of a friend.'

'Sir,' Royer had returned with the concierge, Nolet, 'I have the prisoner.'

'Very good. Bonjour Nolet. I trust you spent a comfortable night?' In truth, he looked as tired as I felt with heavy dark shadows all around his eyes. 'Please, sit.'

He did as he was asked. Royer remained standing at his left shoulder, Ouimet at his right. I remained in my seat at my desk.

'Loparelli, the Italian, where is he?' I began.

'Good morning Inspector,' said Nolet, 'Gianni is a Frenchman. He is from Corsica and if he is gone it is no surprise to me.'

'He is the only member of staff I was unable to interview,' said Ouimet, 'and my enquiries have led me to believe he might be a key witness.'

'Gianni will be hiding. It is a thing they do very well in Corsica. He is not so good at much else. He has some rather individual skills that a few discerning gentlemen appreciate.'

'Are you a discerning gentleman Nolet?' I said.

'I am,' said Nolet.

'Why did he have access to your safe?'

'It was so he could run errands,' said Nolet, 'I found him very trustworthy.'

'Did he help you move the body?'

'Yes, I mean no,' said Nolet.

'What do you mean?' said Ouimet.

'I mean yes, he helped. He is a big man my Gianni, and Georges was well, you saw him, and me? I had a bad hand. What was I to do? I could barely turn a page in my diary, let alone,' he trailed off.

'It is not a good idea to lie to protect others,' I said, 'your story has changed now you know we know about Loparelli. We will discover everything eventually, monsieur Nolet, of that you can be certain.'

Nolet hung his head. 'Please don't hurt him if you find him. He is a good boy really,' he said, 'and if he seems angry it will be because he is scared.'

'We will bear that in mind sir,' I said, 'so do you have anything else to tell us? Loparelli helped you move Sabat and cover up the murder, yes?'

Nolet nodded.

'What else are you not telling us?'

Nolet put his head in his hands.

'Monsieur let me be specific,' I said, 'I would like to know how the kitchen knife that killed Sabat came to be in the room. It is not a usual piece of equipment to be found in a bedroom and so it suggests premeditation.'

I let my words hang over his dropped shoulders as he crouched on his chair.

'Someone took that knife from the kitchen with the sole intent of causing harm,' I said, 'do you know what I think? I will tell you the story of the evening and you can let me know if I am correct. What do you say, Nolet?'

Nolet nodded into his hands.

'Bayeux has a problem. A gambling problem. I have seen it before. It is like a disease that needs to be kept under control in case it breaks out and causes more problems. As we have seen recently, it can be fatal.

'I believe you have gambling debts and these debts have outgrown your ability to service them. You have skimmed the cream from so much of the Hotel du Theatre's commerce and started to thin the milk.

'With Sabat, you saw a quick and easy way to make up the difference, maybe even start again? But you were never built for donkey work were you Nolet? That is why you got Loparelli involved.

'How am I doing so far?'

Nolet nodded and stifled a sob.

'But like I said, dirty work is not for you. You are a middleman, supplying needs and wants for your guests and taking your sous, making your commissions.

'It's not enough and your creditors are impatient and unpleasant people. They turn the screw and you? You end up killing your golden goose.

'How much do you owe the House of Loup?'

Nolet looked up with a start, eyes wide.

'Did he tell you to rob and kill Sabat?' I said,

'No,' muttered Nolet, 'I didn't kill anyone. I won't go to hell. Not me.'

'Then who will?' I said.

Nolet looked me in the eye, his gaze steady, 'You. You will.'

Chapter Sixteen.

'So, what do we do about him, boss?' Mistretta was pacing up and down in front of the fireplace, puffing aggressively on his pipe. 'I could get someone to rough him up or will you let me cut his throat while he sleeps?'

'We will do neither, Mistretta,' said Loup, 'he was simply standing up for whom he has feelings for, thereby exposing his weakness.'

'But he blacked your eye, boss.'

'That he did, but he also showed he has limits. He is sentimental,' said Loup, 'had it been me I would have used a pistol instead of a fist.'

'He was being merciful?'

'No, legal. Bassé wants me either behind bars or swinging from a rope. I can feel it.'

'Then we have to get rid of him,' said Mistretta, 'can you talk to people? They can get us another one like Hautefort. He never bothered us.'

'No. We will manage this one. He got what he wanted last night,' Loup rubbed his chin, 'and we pushed him further than I thought we could. We found his edge, which is a valuable thing.'

'What about the money?'

'He bought off the debt in an entertaining fashion and broke the doctor for us. Vignes will be laughing about that for days,' Loup's eyes narrowed, 'and I think the Inspector might still be persuaded to play again under certain conditions.'

'Are you serious?'

'The house is up on Mortain's debt, so on the whole it was a very profitable night.'

'Sometimes I don't understand your thinking boss,' said Mistretta.

'It's simple. We play the longest game in town and therefore cannot lose.'

'What about Nolet, boss?'

'He needs to stay silent.'

'I can make sure of that.'

'If it helps then be my guest.'

'And the two idiots in the Hole?'

'Leave them another day.'

'And then.'

'If they can be useful, put them to work, if not, you know what to do.'

'Of course,' Mistretta licked his lips then relit his pipe.

'Meanwhile, I shall write our esteemed inspector another invitation, to let him know there are no hard feelings,' Loup winced as his involuntary grin split his bruised face, 'and I need the boy to run a message to the Judge, to warn him of Bassé's skill at the game. He didn't learn that at the commissariat.'

'He's a dark horse,' Mistretta grumbled.

'Call the boy,' said Loup, 'send him to my study.'

He took up his ink and paper and inscribed his note to the Judge, then blew across the page to dry the ink, then folded and sealed the letter with care. When he looked up from his task, he saw Jean, the errand boy, waiting in the doorway.

'Come here,' said Loup, and he offered the letter and a coin to the boy, 'show me your hands,' Loup nodded approval, they were clean enough, 'take this to the Judge. Give it to him personally. Go now and be as quick as you can, then come straight back here to me.'

Jean nodded, saying nothing. He took the petit sou and hid it away, took the letter, and held it tight in his fist. He hesitated a moment, then seeing the look on Monsieur Loup's face he raced out of the room, along the back corridor, and out into the stable yard where old man Fabron was shovelling up warm sweet smelling horse droppings.

Jean slipped through the gate and onto the road. It was cold this morning, much colder than the day before, and there was a breeze that bit through his jacket as if it wasn't there. He shivered and began to run. Running meant he was sure to be warm. It was only cold if he stood still.

When he arrived at the Judge's quarters at the rear of the Palais de Justice, Bernard the porter greeted him with a frown. 'What do you want?' he growled.

143

'The Judge,' said Jean.

'I don't think so,' said the porter.

'I have to give him a letter in person.'

'Really?'

'Yes sir, please?'

'Wait here.'

The porter closed the door, leaving the errand boy to shiver as the cold northerly wind sliced across the street. He shivered and tried to hide inside the stone doorframe, but the wind sought him out, biting at his rags.

As he waited it began to snow, small flakes at first, driven sideways by the insistent wind, but sparkling like tiny stars as they hit the cobblestones. The flakes grew rapidly as the wind dropped. Soon they were piling up across the street, drifting against the doorway. Jean began to lose feeling in his feet and stamped them up and down to keep from freezing.

At last, the porter returned.

'Come in,' said the porter, 'but touch nothing or I will have your fingers off.'

Grateful, Jean obeyed and blew on his hands as he entered the building. He thought for a moment about losing his fingers and rubbed his hands together. Out of the wind and snow, he immediately began to feel warmer. He followed the porter through a kitchen filled with stomach-wrenching aromas but was almost running to keep up with the long-legged old man. In a corner of the kitchen was a narrow door that led to a narrower, enclosed staircase that led directly to the Judge's chambers.

They climbed the servant's stairs quickly, the old porter in front and soft-footed as a burglar. At the top, he pushed open a narrow door onto a palatial corridor. Jean's eyes widened as he took in the gilded woodwork and bright-eyed portraits that glared back at him. The porter knocked at a large, panelled door that smelled of polish.

There was silence for a long moment before they heard the command to enter the room.

'Sir,' said the porter, 'here is the urchin.'

'Thank you, Bernard,' said Judge Tanquerel, resplendent in red velvet, like a Roman Catholic Cardinal.

'Come here boy.'

Jean stepped forward.

'What do you have for me?'

The boy reached into his jerkin, pulled out Loup's letter, and passed it to the Judge.

'Thank you. Wait here both of you,' he opened the note and slowly looked over the contents, then began to laugh until he had to wipe his eyes.

'Oh dear, poor fellow,' he chuckled, 'beaten? About time too. Now wait a moment please while I compose a reply,' The judge's eyes hardened for a moment, 'no, get this boy something from the kitchen Bernard, there's a good fellow, and return in say, half an hour? I will have the reply ready by then.'

'Very good sir,' said the porter. Jean followed as he left the room.

The Judge took the note over to his desk and picked up paper and pen.

'Dear sir,' he began, 'be assured that I esteem your judgement in many things for you are a born connoisseur, however, I should have to let you know that our new man is from a fine and distinct line of magicians and illusionists. I do apologise as I feel I really should have let you know. I realise now, of course, that this is important information, and I should have shared it with you sooner. In my defence, the appointment was made more rapidly than usual, and I could not have predicted that he might seek you out after such a little while. He has not been in post a week. Perhaps next time you will be more prepared. Yours, as ever.'

He did not sign the document. There was no need. He let the ink dry slowly and then folded and sealed the paper.

It was certainly problematic that Bassé had discovered and targeted Loup so soon, but it appeared to be a personal matter for now. If it went any further then perhaps he might have to intervene, but until then Tanquerel felt that it may be that Bassé had done them all a favour, knocking some of the

145

wind out of Loup's sails. Loup needed to remember he had a place in the scheme of things and that he should stick to it.

'I will have to remind the man of his debt to me,' mused the Judge, gazing out through his window toward the twin spires of the cathedral. 'We cannot have so many demands on the future that nothing is realised.'

There was a knock at his door.

'Yes?' and the door opened.

'Sir, I have the papers for today's business,' said a clerk.

'On my desk please Rabuteau.'

'Yes sir.'

'Anything of interest today?' said the Judge.

'Nothing unusual.'

'Good thing too, unusual cases upset my appetite,' the Judge looked up, 'dismissed.'

As the clerk left the porter returned.

'Let me send the urchin on his way,' said Tanquerel, 'here is his letter.'

'Yes sir.'

'Did you feed the boy?'

'Yes sir.'

'Good. He needs to know his loyalties lie with the law. Give him something to take home.'

The porter hurried back to the kitchen where he found Jean being fussed over by a kitchen girl. The boy's cheeks were flushed with warmth, and something moved the porter to soften.

'Boy,' he said, 'I have your letter, but the weather has turned bad out. You must wait indoors until it gets better. Perhaps an hour, but no longer.'

Jean nodded, taking the envelope.

'Wrap him some bread and cheese,' said Bernard to the kitchen girl, then to Jean. 'Remember who it is that you work for, boy.'

Bernard left them to it. Inside the kitchen, it was very warm. The ovens were up and running, fires banked up and lunch was well underway. Through the high windows, Jean and the girl could see snow being blown this way and that.

146

'It looks very cold outside,' said the kitchen girl, 'if I had my way, I wouldn't go out at all until spring. I would be perfectly happy looking after the fires here in the kitchen all winter long if they would let me. Of course, it is different in the summer, but it's still never warm enough for me. What about you? You don't seem to be bothered much by the cold.'

Jean shrugged.

'Let me find you some bread and cheese. What's your favourite? We have all sorts here. The Judge loves his cheese. He likes the camembert of course, who doesn't? But he has cheeses sent up from the mountains down by Spain. He had one that was covered in brown wax. It looked nasty but he liked it so much he makes sure to order it every Michaelmas. It didn't look very nice to me.

'Don't worry,' she went on, 'we've got some good and ordinary farm cheese in the pantry. It won't make you ill.'

Jean nodded.

'You don't say much do you?'

Jean shrugged in reply and watched as she disappeared into the pantry. All around him, the kitchen staff bustled away, oblivious to his presence. He liked that. Invisibility was his special skill. Not to be noticed was his aim. He found the kitchen girl making him the centre of her attention difficult at first, but she seemed nice.

When she returned the girl had a parcel wrapped in sackcloth.

'My name is Agnes,' she said, 'what's yours?'

'Jean,' he said.

'So you can talk,' she said, 'you know, I could ask here for you. Maybe get you a job here in the kitchens? I never go hungry. It's hard work, but I like it.'

'I must go,' said Jean, 'thank you for the food.'

'You're welcome,' Agnes watched as Jean trotted away in the direction of the porter's door. She was not much older than the street boy, perhaps a year or two, and something about him had made her feel less alone. The kitchen was a busy place to spend any amount of time and there was always shouting and noise and clatter, but there were few others here close to her own age.

Agnes sighed and made her way over to the sink where a pile of washing up waited for her. High above her head, she could see the snow blowing about, greying the light, and dampening her spirits. She thought about Jean running through the blizzard over frozen cobbles. At least it was warm here.

She stretched her arms, then rolled up her sleeves and made a start on the never-ending stacks of Palais de Justice porcelain.

Chapter Seventeen.

I took my rest at the commissariat. Snow was building outside and would cool the heels of any fugitive and delay the thoughts of revenge any of my new enemies might be planning. I made up the fire in the office and settled on the chaise and let sleep come and carry me away. Ouimet and Royer were taking care of the manhunt. As soon as we had the Corsican, I was sure our case would be solved. Nolet might be spared the rope, but Loparelli would not be so lucky. Unfortunately, it also made him more dangerous.

When I awoke it was already dark outside and a wind had picked up, rattling the windows of my office. The fire was still warm, but the sound of the wind still made me shiver. I peered out to see the lamps had been lit and the square blanketed in a thick deposit of snow. Black shapes hurried from point to point, men and women still going about their business. I watched a dog jump up and disappear nose-first into a snow drift. It came out again in an explosive effort, then turned around and jumped back in, on the hunt for something.

I went downstairs to see whether there was any news. Sergeant Leverrier was on the front desk and the commissariat was as quiet as the grave. The weather had been keeping everyone inside, seemingly out of trouble.

'Sir,' said Leverrier, 'Mademoiselle Foucher is here in the better interview room again.'

'Thank you, Sergeant.'

The reporter was buried in a vast coat still dusted with snow. Her face was bright pink with the cold.

'Mademoiselle, good evening.'

'Good evening Inspector,' she shivered.

I thought then to invite her up to my office, where the fire could be quickly revived but decided it prudent to find out her business first.

'To what do I owe this visit?'

'I have been busy observing the various comings and goings in the city and taken advantage of the fact that I am currently unknown to most.'

'It is a small city, Mademoiselle Foucher. You will not keep your secret for long.'

'What, sir, is your interest in a certain Monsieur Loup?'

'His establishment attracts criminals, and as criminals are my business, that should explain my interest.'

'Did you know that his name was mentioned more than once in the courthouse in Rouen?'

'I must confess, I did not. To what end was he spoken of?'

'He has business interests in Rouen. Quite legitimate, but they do appear to attract the criminal classes.'

'Should I be concerned about this Loup?'

'You tell me, Inspector,' she shivered again, this time sending a tiny cascade of snow onto the floor, 'after all, you were there on Thursday night.'

'Come upstairs to my office,' I was decided, 'there is a fire. We can talk more freely.'

I indicated the door and thought I noticed a brief hesitation on her part, but she nodded and let me lead the way.

My office was warm, but I added coal to ensure the temperature remained liveable. I helped Mademoiselle Foucher out of her coat, and she settled in a chair close to the fire. I sat opposite, not behind my desk. I didn't want this to be a formal interview.

'I am well aware Mademoiselle Foucher,' I began.

'Call me Angèle, please.'

'Very well, Angèle. I am aware that reporters can be useful regarding investigations,' she smiled at me then and her face lit up as if her corporeal being had, all at once, been inhabited by an actual angel. 'So please, hold nothing back that you feel might be of use to either me or the investigating magistrate. In return, I would be happy to speak to you first at the successful conclusion and prosecution of a crime.'

Her smile vanished as fast as it had appeared.

'You don't understand Inspector,' she adopted an even more crestfallen look, 'I don't want to write about the past. I want to write about the present.'

'Indeed,' I thought quickly, 'so let us make a deal. Tell me what you know about this Loup fellow, and I will see what I can do.'

I got up and crossed to my desk and picked up some paper. It was time to open a dossier on Loup.

'Tell me everything Angèle,' I said.

'What should I call you?'

'You may call me Inspector,' I said, 'for now.'

Mademoiselle Angèle Foucher spoke for perhaps forty minutes, reading from a notebook. She had her own dossier.

'If I may say so, Angèle, you do appear to be incredibly interested in a man who you say was simply mentioned in court in Rouen as a business owner,' I watched her eyes flicker before she looked up from the page, 'is there some personal motivation? It would not be wrong if that were the case.'

'My motivation is simply that no one else has noticed,' she said, 'and that if there is a story that needs to be told then I want to be the one who tells it.'

'I hope you have plenty of patience in store. These things can take time to uncover.'

'I realise that Inspector. I can wait. Now what were you doing there the other night? I have to say that the evening ended in a most satisfying if surprising manner.'

'I had a personal matter to attend to.'

'Do you always use stage theatrics?'

'Only when necessary.'

'Now, you see, any of my colleagues on Le Matin might have revelled in the chance to write such a story about the city's new police Inspector, but me,' she winked, 'I know no one would have believed it.'

'Indeed,' what else could I say?

'So do you have something else I could write about, to help cement me in my role in my first few days on the paper?'

'I do; indeed, I do,' for in that moment I had decided how I could turn this into an advantage, 'I should let you know that I do not believe we have apprehended the killer, that our murderer is still at large. We have identified our man and do not expect that the public is in any danger and are confident of an imminent arrest.'

It was time to put the pressure on and see if it had any effect. I would have to brief Ouimet, and Royer too, should they return empty-handed from their search. If they apprehended our suspect, then all would be well.

'Does this mean that the concierge of the Hotel du Theatre will be released?'

'Not a decision for me to make. There is evidence that the man we arrested, Monsieur Nolet, is complicit. We will put everything we have in front of the judge very soon and then you shall have your answer.

'For now, do you have enough?'

'I do Inspector, thank you.'

'And have you warmed through?'

'I have.'

I stood and took down her coat from where I had hung it and helped her fold herself back into it. She took my arm, and I walked her out to the front steps of the commissariat. The snow was falling with less conviction now and glowed orange in the lamplight.

'Thank you, Inspector. I will see you again soon. Good night.'

'Good night, Mademoiselle.'

I stood for a moment on the steps to the commissariat and pondered this surprising woman. The revelation that she had been surveying Loup's gambling house when I had been inside playing cards had come as a shock. It had been a risk, taking Loup up on his invitation, but being spotted by a member of the press was not something I had thought of. I would have to take better account of this ambitious reporter in the future.

I decided to pay a visit to the cells. The cold might have made Nolet more talkative. As I made the descent, I could feel the chilly air rise up to meet me. It felt colder than usual, but everything here was colder than the tropics.

I heard someone coughing in the first cell at the bottom of the stairs. One of our regular vagrants. At least in here, he would be spared the winter wolf of Bayeux, the slow twin horror of death by hunger and by freezing. Opposite was the gaoler's office. I could smell his coffee pot simmering on the stove. I decided to look in on him.

'Michel? Hello.' I knocked on his door and pushed it open.

'Commissaire?' he said and started to get up. I motioned for him to stay seated.

'A quiet day Michel?'

'Yes sir. A few tramps wanting a night out of the wind is all, and your murderer. I looked in on them,' he squinted at a clock on the wall, 'an hour ago.'

'Good,' I said, 'I will check again.'

'Of course, sir.'

'I will go on my own. No need to get up.'

'Take some coffee with you, sir, it's cold down here.'

'Thanks, Michel.'

I took a tin cup of oil-black coffee in both hands and started down the corridor. In the big communal cell, a half dozen ragged men sat bunched together on an old straw mattress. They were barely distinguishable from each other as individuals, each having had their unique being boiled down to this essential husk. I often wondered who they had been before they lost everything that marked them out as someone's son or brother. In the summer you saw them sleeping in hedgerows, in winter they were hidden away in barns.

At the far end of a row of single cells was the quiet, safe billet we had given Nolet. Here he would be spared the sport and catcalls of the thugs and drunkards we usually saw at the weekend. The church tells us time for solitary contemplation is precious and to be treasured, leading to a deeper understanding of the ultimate truths handed down by the church fathers. Too much of it was likely to send a person like Nolet insane.

I knocked on the cell door and then slid open the viewing panel. Nolet was curled up on the old grey mat that passed for a bed. A rough blanket was drawn tight around his shoulders. I felt a pang of sympathy for the man who had been living in the civilised world until very recently. Stripped of his position, and his influence, he was suddenly shrunken, diminished.

The feeling was short-lived. He had shown no remorse, only concern that his accomplice may come to harm. Too late for that.

I sipped my coffee. I felt it hit the back of my throat. The sudden heat made me emit a low growl. Nolet twitched, becoming smaller in his grubby nest. I repeated the noise, with more aggression and watched as Nolet shuddered.

'I did not say anything, I swear,' he muttered, 'he doesn't know anything.'

I tried for a third growl, but it stuck in my throat, and I coughed instead. Nolet sat upright and backed against the wall, eyes wild.

'What don't I know, Nolet?' I said.

'I don't know,' said Nolet, 'I don't know anything, so I can't tell you anything.'

'So you keep saying,' I said, 'but as I keep reminding you, we will discover everything in due course. You could save me some time and I could help you.'

'If you do discover everything you will wish you had not.'

'I will take my chances, Nolet. You, on the other hand, are fast running out of options.'

'No Inspector, I have none. I must accept my fate. I must go to prison.'

'Indeed, you must,' I said, 'but how do you think you will survive? How many years? What is a tolerable number? Five? Ten? Twenty?'

'No Judge would give me twenty years,' said Nolet, 'certainly not Tanquerel.'

'You might be right, but I could ask the Prefect to have you tried in Caen or perhaps Rouen. In Rouen it is likely they would hand you twenty-five or transportation.'

'You don't know that' said Nolet, 'I have a lawyer.'

'Good. Then ask your lawyer what he thinks of the court at Rouen. He will agree with me.'

'You can't do that.'

'I can send you to trial wherever I think it best. In fact, I am inclined to begin the paperwork tonight and get you on your way,' I narrowed my eyes, 'out of my police station for your own safety.'

'What?'

'Keep you out of harm's way,' I said, 'Sabat had a lot of friends here. Some of them were not nice people.'

'Please?'

'They play rough in Bayeux Nolet. It would be nice to keep you alive long enough to hang.'

'I can't go to Rouen.'

'Why not Nolet? Is your life worth more than that of a travelling salesman?' I slid the viewing panel closed. I had a bad aftertaste in my mouth from the coffee grounds. I turned and stalked back to the gaoler's office.

As I walked past the cell full of tramps, I gave them a quick look. They were all so similar, gaunt, and vacant-eyed, clothes, skin, and hair greyed by weather. I tapped on the bars of their cage but got no response. They reminded me of a truck full of bears I had seen many years ago when I was still a boy. A travelling show from somewhere past the Ural Mountain range had crossed our path one day. I remember someone saying the bears were Chinese. They sat collected in a heap of mangy fur, eyes glazed as if they were already dead, although you could see the rise and fall of their breathing.

Depressed, I walked away. I wondered how much colder it was outside. I had forgotten how chilly Normandy could get in winter. There was a little warmth coming out of Michel's room.

'We need to heat the cells,' I said.

'What's that sir?'

'We need to heat the cells. It is too cold down here.'

'It's not a hotel sir.'

'Pardon?'

'It's dry and out of the wind.'

'Yes constable, but it is very cold tonight,' I said, 'go to the stores and get Nolet another blanket at least.'

'If you say so sir, you're the boss. Do you want more coffee?'

'Thank you,' I said, 'now, the vagrants.'

'What about them sir? You want me to give them blankets too?'

'Of course, and breakfast.'

'How's that sir?'

'I want them fed,' I said, 'do they have names?'

'Only those I give them, sir.'

'And what do you call them?'

'Jean.'

'All of them?'

'Yes sir, trust me. It's easier that way.'

I drank the coffee down more quickly than I meant to and got another gritty mouthful of grounds. Michel spotted my grimace.

'It's rough but it works its magic,' he said.

'Keep an eye on our murderer, monsieur Nolet,' I said, 'I fear he is not in a good way.'

'I will go and get the blankets right away sir,' he said, 'don't you worry, they'll all be right as rain.'

'Thank you, Michel,' I climbed the stairs to my office. Here the fire was still warm. I sighed and felt myself relax, crossed to the fireplace, and topped it up with a handful of coals. As I warmed up, walking up and down the room, I spotted that my pile of paperwork had grown. With a grunt of satisfaction, I settled in my chair, flexed my signing fingers, and started going through the never-ending stack of statements, demands, orders et cetera that are required to run a well-ordered world. Each sheet of paper, in its small way, helps to hold back the tide of chaos that crashes at the door every day and keeps the lords of misrule at bay.

The rhythm of the minutiae of administration calmed me down in the same way a priest's monotone drowns out the worries of his flock.

There came an urgent knocking on my door, breaking me out of my reverie. Ouimet came in.

'Nice and warm in here sir,' he said, stomping over to the fireplace, leaving a trail of snow in his wake.

'Cold out.' I observed.

156

'Freezing,' said Ouimet, 'and no sign of our man. Likely he has gone to ground. There's not many folks out in this weather tonight.'

'Snow keeps 'em quiet,' snorted Sergeant Royer, following Ouimet into the room, 'but it can hide every sin you can think of.'

'We will discover them in the thaw,' I said.

'When did you last see snow sir,' said Royer, 'must have been some time ago? It doesn't snow in the jungle does it?'

'A long time Sergeant, nearly ten years,' I said, 'Sometimes even the rain was warm in the jungle.'

'Pardon me, but that's not natural,' said Royer.

'Rain is natural,' said Ouimet, 'no matter what the temperature is.'

'No sign then gentlemen?' I said, 'No one saw or heard anything?'

'Sorry, no,' said Ouimet, 'nothing at the railway station or the hotel.'

'What about the rotten shack where we found Sabat?'

'I will look in the morning,' said Ouimet.

'Don't go on your own,' I said, 'take a couple of constables with you. He might well be armed.'

'Of course, I'll take Desnier and the new man,' said Ouimet, 'that Desnier is good in a scrap.'

'I'll let them know,' said Royer.

Both men stood in front of my fire, blocking the heat but I did not mind. I was warm enough by now.

'Michel is grumbling, you made him a nurse to his guests down in the cells,' said Royer.

'That's right Sergeant,' I said, 'can you bring them some fresh bread in the morning?'

'Be happy to,' said Royer, stomping back out of the room.

'Where are you going Sergeant?' I said.

'Sorry sir,' Royer recovered himself and turned around. He was still getting used to the new situation.

'That's better,' I said, 'and tomorrow morning I want you to go to Loup's club and make general inquiries regarding Loparelli.

157

Make it known we regard Nolet as an innocent man caught up in events.'

'Is he?' asked Ouimet.

'Not at all,' I said, throwing Ouimet a look, 'but we have to push in all directions and pull at every loose thread to get a result. Most of all we need Loparelli.'

'We'll find him, sir,' said Ouimet, 'if he's not in the hut I think it's likely he may be closer to home.'

'At the hotel?'

'Perhaps in the theatre.'

'You follow it up Ouimet,' I said, 'and I will have another chat with our concierge. He might be more talkative with some warm bread in his stomach tomorrow morning.'

'Another log on your fire?' asked Ouimet.

'What? No. No thank you, Ouimet,' I said, 'I should start sleeping at home.'

Ouimet made a face. 'It will be cold though sir. The snow is halfway to my knees already.'

'I don't want to stay here. I really don't,' I said. I had journeyed through snow before, and I would do it again. 'I expect my housekeeper has already made up my fire, and it is not so far away.'

'Very well,' said Ouimet.

'Indeed,' I said, 'good work today gentlemen. Go home too. I will see you in the morning.'

'Good night sir,' said Ouimet and Royer.

'Goodnight gentlemen,' I said.

Part of me regretted my decision as I strode out into the cold, wet, dark night, but when I turned the key in the door, I could feel the warmth of the house and caught the aroma of a fine mutton stew awaiting my attention.

Chapter Eighteen.

I shut my eyes to sleep, and it only seemed like a moment later that the peculiar snow-bright light was illuminating my sleeping quarters like a frozen midday summer sun. The light was hard and had a glacial solidity. I rubbed my eyes and tried to focus on the clock on the wall. It was late. I had slept well. No dreams.

I hurried about my morning toilet and left for the commissariat without refreshment. I would make coffee at work.

The pavement was icy and treacherous beneath my boots and there was still no sign of a thaw. Snow had drifted and hardened, reflecting the cold sun.

I stormed across the commissariat to the stairs to my office. The building was filled with the aromas of coffee and woodsmoke. Someone had already lit the fire in my office, for which I was grateful. As I took my chair there was a knock on the door behind me.

'Come in,' I said.

'Good morning sir,' said Royer.

'Good morning,' I replied.

'I have coffee and a pastry for you, sir,' said Royer, 'two pastries.'

'Two? What happened?'

'I had some left over from the guests in the donjon sir,' he said.

'No,' I shook my head, the light was so bright I could see every mote of dust in the room, 'no Royer, that's not it.'

'Not what sir?'

'Don't play the fool with me Sergeant, what's going on?'

'Well, we have good news and bad this morning.'

'Spit it out.'

'Ouimet found Loparelli, where you said to look too,' said Royer, 'he went out to that old shack at dawn and there he was.'

'Dead?'

'As you like, sir,' said Royer, 'that's the bad news.'

'Damn it.'

'Deputy Ouimet is still there waiting for the doctor. He asked if you could take a look at the scene before they moved him.'

I sipped my coffee. It was the perfect temperature. I dipped the end of a croissant into the cup, tore it off, and put it in my mouth, chewing slowly, chewing over this new information.

'I have a carriage ready for you,' said Royer, eyeing me nervously. I was no longer the young cadet he had first known more than a decade ago. I was someone else now and he was realising how much he had to get to know who I had become since then.

'Good,' I said, 'thank you Royer. Tell the driver I will be there in five minutes.' It might have been simpler for me to take up a role in a different city. I had considered it. One had been offered, but when the chance arrived to take on Bayeux, I had no second thoughts.

I dismissed the sergeant with a wave of my hand. My blood was coming up. I could feel it rise slowly. I counted, breathed. Loparelli, dead. What a disappointment. But even though a wise superior had once said to me, 'The dead are never in a hurry,' I could not afford to take my time over my coffee.

The city's roads were busy despite the snow. Commerce continued whatever the weather when there were sous to be made. The mayor had sent out his teams early to clear the drifts and to keep the main roads passable.

Royer sat next to me in silence. I wondered what he thought of my appointment. I was so wet behind the ears at eighteen, yet I thought I knew it all and would change the world with my insight. It was a wonder to me that I could go away for a decade or more only to find the sergeant basically unchanged. He was a man set in his ways, that is for certain, and his ways had likely served him well. It is the normal way of things for a man or woman to find a role that suits them and settle into it for a lifelong journey. Perhaps I might have put the travelling and change behind me. Was I more like my father, my grandpa or Sergeant Royer?

I do not have the answer, but I do know that it is good to have something to do.

'What are you thinking about Royer?' I asked.

'Sorry sir?' said Royer.

'You seem deep in thought,' I said, 'I am sorry to interrupt you.'

'No, no, that's alright sir,' he said, 'I was just thinking about the murders. We don't get many around here. That is, we didn't used to, not like this. It used to be it was an easy thing to find a murderer, but these killings, I don't know.'

'I see,' I said, 'it is difficult sometimes. In Paris, life was cheap. In Guyana, cheaper still. I'm afraid the sickness may be spreading.'

The carriage came to a halt. Ahead of us was the infirmary wagon, the doctor just stepping down into the knee-deep snow.

'Let's go,' I said, then called out a greeting to the doctor who waited for us to catch up.

'Good morning Doctor. Here we are again.'

'Coincidence?' said the doctor.

'Hardly,' I said, 'this is sending a message.'

'Who to?' said Royer.

'Let's go and find out,' I said, 'there's Ouimet.'

We followed a well-trod path through the snow to where Ouimet and the two constables waited. The door to the shack was laid to one side, the brambles describing crystalline white loops that sparkled in the icy sunshine.

I clapped my hands together and rubbed them hard against the chill of the air.

'So, Loparelli?' I said to Ouimet.

'Yes sir, it would seem so,' said Ouimet.

'Identification?'

'There were papers on him,' Ouimet handed over a carefully folded document.

'Thank you,' I put the papers in an inside pocket for later study then advanced through the open door.

There he was. Our man. Laid out on his back in a cruciform arrangement and barefoot. I took a step back.

'This is why you wanted me here,' I said.

Royer and Ouimet both nodded.

'I would have been upset to have not been called,' I said, 'It would indeed appear to be a message. Doctor?'

'Yes?'

'Check for a single stab wound to the heart.'

'Let me take a look at the gentleman,' Doctor Richelieu pushed his way inside the hovel and began a cursory examination. 'Young chap, not more than twenty-five I'd say. Not very tall, but then he is quite clearly not a Norman. Here, under the coat, is the wound you mentioned.'

'Are you certain?' I said.

'Yes,' said Richelieu, 'you were correct. A single stab wound to the heart. Perfectly executed. A quick, quiet death at first glance, but.'

'But what?'

'Less blood than I would have expected,' said Richelieu, 'not like your last customer. Interesting. I will tell you more after I have had a better look.'

'Thank you, Doctor,' the dead man was pale as snow, his hair black as shadow. He looked like a tintype of the person he used to be. Something about him stirred a memory. I was not certain, but I thought perhaps I had seen this man before, perhaps at the hotel.

'Ouimet?' I said.

'Yes sir?'

'We need to establish exactly when Loparelli was last seen alive. Doctor, if there is nothing more we can do for this fellow I would like him in the dead room before too long.'

Doctor Richelieu nodded assent.

'Ouimet, can you bring in Madame Omer to identify this boy once your enquiries are complete? We have to be sure.'

'We have Nolet at the commissariat,' said Ouimet, 'we could use him.'

'Nolet is a liar and not to be relied upon, but a housekeeper can usually be trusted,' I said, 'and we have to be certain this man is who his papers say he is.'

'Well, Nolet didn't kill this one,' said Ouimet, 'so someone is following in his footsteps for a reason. Why?'

I shrugged. 'This is bigger than Nolet, Sabat or Loparelli,' *or even Mortain come to that*, I thought. Mortain was a hidden murder and would have stayed undiscovered had the ice not slowed the flow of the river. Sabat's murder was as savage as any other, the disposal, however, was simple laziness, the inability perhaps to solve the problem of the frozen river and the stone-hard fields.

'I wonder how many others were sent to sea via the river. This? This killing is perhaps a warning. We must be on our guard gentlemen.'

'How long has he been dead Doctor?' asked Ouimet.

'Hard to say in this weather,' said Richelieu, 'could have been a day or two before he was put here.'

'Like Sabat?' said Ouimet.

'Exactly,' I said, 'Like Sabat before him this man was killed somewhere else before being dumped here. He was dragged and dropped in almost exactly the same spot. Look at his heels, the skin is raw. Now look at the ground, hardly a spot of blood.'

'I don't like it,' said Royer, 'it's not a normal murder.'

'My question is Sergeant, who knew the circumstances in which we found Sabat? Apart from me, you, our men, and the doctor's staff,' I paused, 'the farmer's boy? No. That is enough for the story to spread wide enough.'

'If Loparelli has been killed and dumped in the same way that he did for Sabat,' Ouimet said, 'is it someone sending Nolet a message? Punishment for being sloppy?'

'I don't know, could be. In which case we have a serious problem,' I said, 'It's what I might expect in Le Havre or Rouen, but not here. What we need next is a positive identification and a search of Loparelli's quarters as quickly as possible. As soon as the doctor has cleared him away, nail that door back in place Sergeant.'

'Right you are, sir,' said Royer.

'It will let whoever left him there understand that we don't expect it to happen again,' I said, 'Ouimet, you and I need to pay a visit to the Hotel du Theatre.'

The sky was already beginning to darken as we trudged back across the hardened snow. The sun had disappeared behind the serried ranks of heavy clouds. More snow was coming to cover the tracks of our murderer, our hunter, this new winter wolf with its legendary appetite.

I climbed back into the carriage and discovered my pain au chocolat in the pocket of my coat. I took it out. It was square and compressed quite flat. It tore easily. I chewed and thought and waited while Ouimet slowly caught up. The last piece was gone when he climbed through the door. I knocked on the ceiling and called out our destination to the driver. We moved off at once.

'Why do you think they killed him?' said Ouimet.

'Who?'

'Loparelli.'

'Because they could not get to Nolet,' I said, 'but they know he will hear of it and get the message. If he talks to us then his fate is sealed, but then again, I do not believe he will last long in the penitentiary.'

'What is stopping him from taking them all down with him?' said Ouimet, 'A final act of revenge?'

'There will be some insurance along the way. A relative or some other interest,' I said, 'he might be supporting family elsewhere. It could all be put at risk. Better he stays silent to protect his legacy.'

'Do you think this Loparelli was responsible for the death of the man found in the river last week?' said Ouimet, 'I'm not certain that the good doctor spent too much time with him.'

'The river has taken any number of the dead out to sea,' I said, 'so many the town should consider changing the name of the Aure to the river Styx.'

'The what?'

'It is the river in ancient mythology that separates the world of the living from the world of the dead.'

'I see.'

'And it has been taking the dead on their final journey for some time. Sergeant Royer was complaining that murder used

164

to be a simple business. I suppose it was when all the complicated murders were being sent out to sea.'

'Is that what it was like in Paris?'

'Remind me, where are you from Ouimet?'

'Laval,' he rolled his eyes, 'it's in the Mayenne, on the way to Angers I suppose, but there's not much there.'

'Why the Police?'

'I wanted to get out and see something of the world, not all of it,' he said, 'not like you, but enough.'

'Is Bayeux enough?'

'Today, sir, I would have to say yes,' he said, 'more than enough. Nothing ever happened in Laval. I had my education, and I was expected to be apprenticed to a Notaire or study to be an accountant, but numbers aren't people, no matter how much people need accountants.'

'An interesting logic Ouimet,' I said.

'What about you sir,' said Ouimet, 'if you don't mind my asking. The men have been talking about how your father was on the stage in Paris and we all wonder why you chose this path instead?'

'It's something to do, Ouimet, something to do.'

Chapter Nineteen.

At the hotel, the staff were preparing for the midday meal. The building was warm, and the place was lit with a brittle light as if the air was about to snap. The man at the desk, Chevrolet greeted us with a tired smile.

'I should thank you Commissaire, that our hotel is half full, now I am working in both the day and the night. It has made it easier.'

'I am certain you will do a most professional job, Monsieur,' I said, 'now if you allow, we would like to speak with your housekeeper, Madame Omer.'

'Of course, I will send for her,' he said.

'We would also like to look at Giancarlo Loparelli's quarters.'

'Who?'

'Loparelli. He is a night porter of yours. Tall, stocky, dark fellow,' I said, 'a friend of Nolet's.'

'You mean Gianni?'

'Yes, that's him.'

'He works at the theatre. Lives in the attic over the stables,' said Chevrolet, 'very shy. Rarely seen.'

'When was the last time you saw him?' said Ouimet.

'About a month ago,' said Chevrolet, 'he was standing out the back smoking his pipe in the dark. Well, there was some moonlight I suppose, and it was strange...'

'Strange how,' said Ouimet.

'It was the coldest night, but he was stripped to the waist,' he grunted, 'Corsicans. Strange people I think, tough people.'

'Thanks,' said Ouimet.

'Let's go,' I said to Ouimet. He nodded.

'You still want to see the housekeeper?' said Chevrolet.

'Later,' I said, 'can we go through the back door?'

'That way sir,' said Chevrolet.

We went through a narrow door at the other end of the foyer and ducked along a dimly lit corridor. At the end was a stable door with a window in the top half. It was the kind of door that let in cool air in the summer and kept the yard dogs out. The hotel and theatre shared the stable yard to the rear, and I imagined this doorway was where Chevrolet had spotted the porter that night.

Snow had started falling again. Thick, heavy white petals, obscuring everything, disguising the usual human mess, the back-of-house trash, and leftovers from the front-of-house display.

At one end of the stable block, I thought I could see a thin wisp of smoke rising from a narrow chimney. I pointed it out to Ouimet. He nodded again.

'I see it,' he said, 'what do you want to do?'

'Go and check on the horses,' I said.

I lifted the latch and pushed open the door. A snowdrift had built up in front of it and was almost as high as my knees. I put a finger to my lips and made off into the heavy weather. There was no wind, and the snowflakes were suddenly very thick, piling up on my coat, and getting in my eyes. The kind of snow that would soak you through and then freeze you to death. It crunched beneath our feet as we crossed the courtyard. Only one of the stable doors was open. We headed for it.

There was a low overhang which kept the snow off us as we peered into the gloomy interior of the building. At the other end, there was a flicker of lamplight between the wallboards. The fireplace sending up the tell-tale smoke. I signalled to Ouimet, and we crept along the front of the stable, keeping close under the projecting roof.

When we reached the end door we stopped and I strained to hear whether there was any conversation within, which would betray the numbers to expect. All was silent. I drew my pistol and tapped on the door.

No response, so I tapped again, sharper, louder, then, grabbing the door handle I pulled, swinging the door wide open.

'Police!' I called out, but the room was empty.

The lamp lay on its side, oil spilt over onto a pile of straw. On a low bench, next to a small fire, a tin cup steamed. Fragments of straw floated from the roof beams like indoor snow. I looked up and saw a dark shape making off across the rafters, lit by the flames that were rapidly taking hold of the dry straw. In the next bay a horse whinnied in alarm.

Ouimet dashed past me and beat at the flames with his coat. I turned and tried to catch our fugitive at the other end of the block, but once there I could see or hear no one. He had vanished like a ghost. I went back to help Ouimet with an armful of snow. The fire was almost out. The good deputy had saved the building.

I climbed up onto the bench and pulled myself up into the roof space. Here there was a small platform with a cot piled with straw and blankets. I made a brief survey but there was little in the motley collection of cheap belongings to enlighten me. There was barely room enough to stand, but I found that when I did my eyes alighted on a small wooden box with a carrying strap, the sort that travelling tradesmen would carry with them. On the side that had a latch were the initials G.L. burned into the wood. I steadied myself with one hand on a rafter and took the box from its hiding place with the other.

'Ouimet?'

'Yes, sir?'

'I have something here.'

'What is it?'

'A box, here, let me drop it down to you,' a movement caught my eye.

It might have been a horse switching its tail or tossing its head but something registered, recognizable as a human action. Instinctively I dropped down onto my haunches as a knife blade whistled past my head and shuddered into a timber strut behind me.

'What was that?' said Ouimet.

'Our friend is in the next bay but one,' I called.

I raised my head a little and was in time to see a dark shape climb out over the top of the stable door.

'He's just left. Stop him if you can. I'm coming down.'

I dropped into the stable hand's parlour, full of burned straw and scorched earth, the travelling box over my shoulder. Ouimet stepped back into the shelter.

'Vanished into the snow,' he said, breathing heavily.

'Which way?'

'Toward the street.'

I put my head out of the door and could hardly see a thing. The snow was coming down in a torrent.

'He has to have friends close by,' I said, 'he wouldn't last ten minutes in this.'

'He might not,' said Ouimet, 'he might be hiding out there waiting for us to leave.'

'I don't know,' I said, 'I've got his box of tricks.'

'Whose box?'

'Loparelli's box.'

'But Loparelli is dead,' said Ouimet, 'I found him this morning. You saw him.'

'We saw a dead man,' I said, 'of that, there can be no doubt. If it was our Loparelli, the man we suspect dealt Sabat the fatal blow, then surely these rude quarters should not have been occupied.'

'Who is our dead man?' said Ouimet.

'We must ask Loparelli when we catch him,' I said, 'but first, let's take a minute to open up this box and see whether it can offer us any help.'

The box was simply made and had only a latch and no lock. I set it on the rough bench and prised it open. Inside was a package wrapped in cloth and tied with twine. I undid the knot that held it together and revealed a sizable cache of bank notes and gold coins.

'That's a lot of money for a stable boy,' said Ouimet, 'where on God's earth would he find that much money?'

'I would guess it is Nolet's nest egg, kept safely hidden away in case of whatever misfortune should come along.'

'It nearly went up in smoke,' said Ouimet.

'Indeed,' I said.

'What shall we do with it?' said Ouimet.

'Put it back where I found it perhaps?' I said, tying the package up, 'No,' I answered my own question, 'you go and see if you can track him. I will be right behind you.'

'What? As you say, sir,' Ouimet made off into the thick waterfall of snow, 'he went this way,' he called.

169

I tossed the box up into the rafters just above the bench. It looked like we had simply abandoned it. Then I went out after my deputy, limping slightly as if I had landed badly, taking a gamble that we were being observed. I guessed that as soon as our man had decided the coast was clear he would return for his prize.

I caught up with Ouimet out on the main street that ran beside the theatre. We were the only two people out on the road that I could see. Visibility was appalling. We could hardly see across the street.

'Which way Ouimet?' I said, 'Hotel or Theatre?'

'Theatre,' he said.

'Why?'

'Not so many regular employees,' he said, 'and a lighter level of staff at this time of day.'

'I like your thinking,' I said, 'and if I were him, I would keep a lookout to see where we were going.'

'I disagree,' said Ouimet, 'with all that money hidden away I would bet he is cutting back in the hope he hasn't lost it all.'

'You could be right,' I said, 'under cover of all this snow. You cut through the theatre, and I will double back. Shoot him if you must. He could have more knives.'

'I'll do my best sir,' Ouimet grinned, 'see you in a few minutes.' He struggled off up the road, kicking snow ahead of him. It thinned a little so I could see Ouimet turn the corner. When he vanished, I made my way slowly back to the entrance to the stable yard. I crouched down in the snow by a stack of empty crates. To my right was the door to the hotel kitchens. It was open and a yellow lamplight spilled out into the snow. I could smell the aromatic gravies the chef had been serving up and my stomach growled. To my left was the stable block almost as we had left it. Now snow was piling up inside the open door. No one had been anywhere near since we had left it.

I kept as still as I could while I waited. The cold did not bother me quite as much as the mesmeric murmuration of the snowflakes that swirled around in front of me. I ignored them and kept my focus on the matter at hand.

A gunshot broke me from my stupor. The echo rebounded and sent a small avalanche off the stable roof. Another round was fired. I left my position and hopped and ran through the ever-deepening snow. I was halfway across the yard when our fugitive came into view. He was holding a revolver at arm's length, pointed back the way he had come. Ouimet had been right and confirmed how desperate this man was.

'Police,' I shouted, 'put down your weapon.'

In response, our quarry turned and sent a bullet flying past my right ear. I pulled the trigger and hit him square in the chest. A second later a bullet from Ouimet's gun split his neck, and our man was down, staining the white snow crimson.

'Are you hit, Inspector?' Ouimet surged into view, his great wide legs ploughing a vast furrow in the snow.

'Well enough, you?'

'Alive.'

'Good, glad you made it,' I said, 'now let us get this devil into the stable and out of the way.'

We took an arm each and dragged him into the parlour where we dropped him on the hard-packed earth, arms spread wide. I reached up and took down the money box. Ouimet recovered the pistol and a few minutes later we were in the dining room of the Hotel du Theatre, warming up with good, hot coffee awaiting the arrival of the doctor.

Chapter Twenty.

At the commissariat all was quiet. The coffee pot was working harder than anyone else. Sergeant Royer was at the front desk, his whiskers damp and dark brown from the drink, they were white at the roots. He seemed a little agitated.

'What's on your mind, Sergeant?' I said.

'Our victim in the old shack this morning,' he said, 'I saw him onto the doctor's wagon and there came this nasty smell off him. So then the doctor cut off his trouser leg. That is, the dead man's trousers, and he had a nasty wound down there.'

'What sort,' I said.

'Doctor Richelieu said it looked like a gunshot, but there was so much nasty pus and the like I could hardly look at it, and the smell,' Royer gasped, 'I thought that dead whale was bad.'

'We've another one for the good doctor,' I said, 'and I am reasonably certain that this one is the real Giancarlo Loparelli.'

The sergeant's eyes widened and almost fell out as I brought him up to date. After I had finished, I called Ouimet and together we went to speak to Nolet.

'Good afternoon,' I said, through the looking panel in the door, 'we have news for you Monsieur Nolet.'

The man on the cot looked no more than a bundle of rags ready for the fire. How much lower can a man fall? It may not compare to the hotel, but to Devil's Island, this was luxury.

'Get up Nolet,' I said, 'come and talk with me over a cup of coffee and perhaps we can make your fate a discreet affair and you may yet escape the rope.'

'You are an intelligent man Commissaire,' Nolet's voice was a thin whine, 'but you understand nothing of my condition. I am already a dead man, a corpse.'

'Of course, Monsieur,' I said, 'life for the concierge is over. No more the Master of Services and favours taken and given at the Hotel du Theatre. That man is indeed dead and gone.

'But what will you have us do with the cadaver? Would you have it disposed of with the utmost discretion, or paraded in public for the gawkers and the curious?'

'What do you mean?' said Nolet.

'Come upstairs and tell me the truth,' I said, 'confess your sins, or let the newspapers tell the story of your trial.'

'What has happened?'

'It is all over Nolet. We have Loparelli. We have the money. We will find the rest of the evidence we need.' I looked him in the eye, 'I said we would find out everything in the end. Once we have finished searching the hotel and the stables, we will have the story that will end with you and the rope.'

Nolet touched his neck with his right hand.

'But you may yet live,' I said.

'Gianni,' muttered Nolet, 'Gianni is dead, isn't he?'

'I am afraid so.'

'Was it quick?'

'He didn't suffer,' I said, 'but it wasn't my choice. I would have liked him to see justice, to stand before the law.'

'Now he stands before God,' said Nolet, 'it is how it had to be, and I cannot bring shame on his memory.'

'Tanquerel will be your Judge if you come now,' I said, 'or you will find yourself in Rouen in a matter of days. If you are lucky, they will hang you, but I fear they have a Judge there who is fond of sending villains to the tropics.'

'You said coffee?'

'I did,' I said, 'and perhaps a little bread too.'

He was cold and tired and hungry. Such deprivations were not what he was used to. The promise of some relief, however slight, finally broke down Nolet's resistance. We gave him a jug and a bowl of warm water so that he could wash, and a rough, but clean shirt to help him back to himself a little.

It was mid-afternoon before we were set ready for him in my office. Jacques, the stenographer was poised with his pencil and Ouimet, dried off, fed, and warmed up, sat by the fireplace.

Sergeant Royer brought Nolet in and we established the facts of identity, date, and time, and then began our interrogation. Nolet confirmed Loparelli was our killer in the case of Sabat, and that as Mortain had owed Nolet money, the Corsican had killed him on principle.

173

'For Gianni, it was a matter of honour,' explained Nolet, 'Jean had not been able to keep his word, but then he also owed Loup, among others. For Gianni, it was simply how things were done.'

'Is that when Loup called in your debt?' I said, 'When your man killed his man?'

'No, it wasn't like that. I don't owe Loup anything.'

'So why kill Sabat?'

'Money. He had so much of it, and we wanted it,' said Nolet, 'we had waited and waited and saved so much, but it was taking too long, making tips here and there, and we had made a bad loan to Mortain and one or two others.'

'Which others? Were there more victims of Loparelli's honour?' I said.

'A few,' said Nolet, 'Henri Sabat covered our losses and put us back into profit.'

'You say 'we' and 'us' a lot, Nolet,' I said, 'as if the two of you were business partners and murder was simply part of your stock in trade.'

'It was about honour Inspector,' said Nolet, 'surely you can see that? A man without honour is not a man, he is a beast of the field. Sabat was a foul beast, driven by low appetites. What happened to him he should have expected. It is what was deserved.'

'You won't know this but today we discovered a dead man carrying Loparelli's papers,' I said, 'what say you?'

Nolet smiled the smile of a man being told what a fine dog he had. *Clever boy*, he seemed to be thinking.

'He was making himself invisible,' said Nolet, 'but for the snow coming down, as I see it did, he might have been able to.'

'I am curious Nolet,' I said, 'what was the plan? What were you raising money for?'

'We had dreams, me and my Gianni,' Nolet became misty-eyed, 'well, that is to say that I had dreams and Gianni was an enthusiastic supporter.'

'What dreams?'

'Travel, Inspector. We were going to California to build the finest hotel in the entire State, full of style and flavour and the richest guests,' he sighed, 'but for such ambition we needed capital. The money in Gianni's box is just a small part of it. The rest has been deposited somewhere very safe indeed.'

'And now your dreams are ruins,' I said, 'and your Gianni was getting ready to flee when we discovered him.'

'You are wrong Inspector,' said Nolet, 'for last night I had a dream that he was coming for me.'

'I can assure you, Nolet, that will not be happening.'

'He said you would say that, but he will be coming for me all the same, and together we will take our money and leave this country.'

'Loparelli is dead, Nolet,' said Ouimet.

'Are you certain of that?' said Nolet, suddenly very serious, 'The stable boy you killed could have been his cousin,' said Nolet, 'my bet is you shot the wrong man.'

'Perhaps we did,' I said, 'formal identification is yet to take place, but will happen in due course. Until that happens you will remain under lock and key as our guest.'

'Thank you, Inspector.'

'So, for our records monsieur Nolet,' I said, 'you admit being party to the murder of Monsieur Henri Sabat and Monsieur Jean Mortain?'

'I do.'

'Care to name any others on your list?'

'What for?'

'To close dossiers, inform relatives, that sort of thing.'

'Administration?'

'If you like.'

'Very well, there was Adolphus Reese, Frederic Mensonge, Alex David and Gregor Damozanne.'

'Well remembered, Nolet,' I said.

'They take it in turns to visit me at night,' he said, 'I promised to name rooms after them in our hotel in Los Angeles. They were our benefactors.'

'I see,' I said, 'but do you feel any regret, any contrition regarding the deaths of these several men?'

'Oh no Inspector,' said Nolet, 'their lives were only improved by coming to an end.'

175

'I beg your pardon sir?' said Ouimet.

'It is better for them that they are dead,' said Nolet, 'had they lived, their appetites would have continued to ruin things of beauty. Instead, I shall be able to use their money for a greater good.'

'Monsieur Nolet,' I said.

I paused in a silence heavy with disbelief. Jacques's mouth hung open and Royer and Ouimet both looked stunned.

'I must be clear that it is all over for you now. The Judge will read this testimony and decide what must be done, but I am certain that you have lost all rights and privileges of common society and are destined never to walk as a free man again.'

'If that is what you believe Inspector,' said Nolet, 'then I must respect that, but I will be on a train tomorrow, bound for a steamer across the Atlantic to our new life.'

'This interview is over,' I said and stood up, 'Deputy Ouimet, Sergeant Royer, see Nolet to his cell.'

Together Ouimet and Royer propelled Nolet out of his seat and through the office door.

'Jacques,' I said.

'Sir?'

'Get a copy to me as quickly as possible for signature. I need a copy to the Judge before nightfall.'

'Yes, sir.'

'Dismissed.'

Left on my own in my office I crossed to the fireplace and spent some time building up the flames until my face began to sting with the heat. I watched the coals glow with a fierce light and suddenly had the fancy that I should replace my eyes with such blazing bright coals to express the madness buried within the fury that I felt.

I kept my eyes dry in this way as I silently shook. I would put a watch on for Nolet's ghosts all night to make sure not one could return to life to grant him his freedom.

There was a knock on my door. It was Royer with good news from the look of him. The stable lad for the hotel was alive and well and had identified Loparelli's body, as had the chef who had fed him, and the scullery maid who had been in love with

176

him, albeit from a distance. It was almost all over. Jacques brought in the confession. Ouimet had managed to get Nolet to scrawl his name at the bottom of each page. I added my signatures as confirmation of approval and Royer had it dispatched to the Palais de Justice.

But it seemed unreal as if it were happening in a fever dream. Yes, I was tired. It had been a long day and a difficult first week. I had not eaten for hours. With my collar up and my hat pulled down over my ears I made a visit to Guillaume's to see what was left of the day's menu.

I was in luck. There was a seafood soup ready, followed by beef, and a ratatouille, then cheeses and coffee. It settled me well. A feast for one. A feast for a free man.

The snow was still coming down outside, in the dark. It was covering up the sins of men, disguising the obscene with a temporary, false beauty. Who knew what misdeeds would be uncovered by the thaw? Whatever happened, the gendarmerie and the commissariat would be waiting.

The waiter offered me a liqueur with my coffee, but I declined. Instead, I took a slice of gateaux. After all, I reasoned, today we had managed to resolve not just one case, but many others besides, and had done so within a week. An auspicious start.

I raised my coffee cup in a silent toast to Lady Fortune hoping that luck would be in my sails.

As I drained my cup a man arrived at my table.

'Bonsoir Inspector,' he said, 'I am Rabuteau, one of the Judge's men. Sorry to disturb you, but his honour would like to clarify a couple of matters.'

'Bonsoir Monsieur Rabuteau,' I said, 'Judge Tanquerel wants to see me now?'

'He is in his chambers, sir. I have been instructed to bring you back with me as a matter of urgency.'

'Very well,' I paid my bill and set off into the night to the Palais de Justice. The snow was still coming down and the wind was blowing it into drifts in doorways. We picked our way across the square and up the steps to the judge's doors.

177

The building was quiet, but fires still burned, keeping it warm. As we ascended the stairs to the judges' rooms, I caught the scent of stew wafting up from the kitchens below.

'Is the Palais always like this?' I said.

'His honour runs the building like it's a part of his estate,' Rabuteau shrugged. 'We never go hungry.'

At last, we reached the door to Judge Tanquerel's chambers. Rabuteau knocked and pushed it open.

'Inspector Bassé, sir.'

'Very good,' said the judge as he looked up from my report, 'and thank you for coming on such short notice Bassé, but I felt it to be my duty to congratulate you in person regarding the detail contained within your deposition. This is the kind of writing I would expect from a lawyer.

'Also, your swift work dealing with the killer and his accomplice will be recognised at the highest level.'

'I'm flattered, sir,' I said, 'but I'm only sorry I could not catch the murderer alive.'

'What matters is that the case is closed Bassé. I am satisfied that there is nothing more to be done. I will have Nolet transferred in the morning.'

'Transferred where, sir?'

'You don't need to worry about that. There will be other things to occupy you and your men tomorrow, no doubt.'

'And the trial?'

'I'll be in touch, Bassé. Good night.'

Chapter Twenty-One.

'You gun a man down in the street and you have nothing to tell me?' Mademoiselle Angèle Foucher was beside herself. Her eyes blazed with a quiet ferocity that held my full attention. Here was a woman not to be taken lightly.

'Mademoiselle,' I said, 'I must apologise, but my hands are tied by the investigating magistrate.'

'Your tongue is tied more like, sir. I thought we had the beginnings of an understanding.'

She retreated to the window of the interview room and stared out at the still-falling snow. She shivered, perhaps from the chill, perhaps from frustration.

'We did,' I said, 'we do. At least I would like to think that is still the case.'

She turned back to me.

'Then please give me something. At least tell me more than the cheap street chatter.'

I had turned the situation over and over in my mind. Now was not the time for me to make more enemies, but one cannot please everybody.

'There is a game being played in this city,' I said, 'a dangerous game of piquet. I do not know who all the players are yet, and I cannot say how the cards will one day fall. So, all I can tell you is this; that it was the evils of gambling which drove these crimes. It links all of the murders.'

'I was right,' said Angèle, 'Loup is implicated.'

'Not directly, so please do not point the finger, not yet. We must be patient and draw him out. Let him think we are none the wiser, that he is smarter, that he is safe.'

'I can do that.'

'Merci Mademoiselle, and when he makes his mistake, which he will, we will have him.'

*

179

Judge Tanquerel drew deep on his pipe, making the tobacco crackle in its bowl. He looked over at Mayor Gevrol who was reading the last page of the dossier sent over by the new Commissaire of Bayeux Police. Gevrol read while holding his left hand half raised as if he was ready to point or call on his tutor for help. At last, he looked up and met Tanquerel's gaze and pointed at him.

'A thorough but succinct account that presents unvarnished detail. I like it,' said Mayor Gevrol, 'however, it manages to make for uncomfortable reading all the same. The city he describes is not the Bayeux I live in Tanquerel.'

'I know just what you mean, Your Excellency,' crooned the Judge, 'you are quite right.'

'What can we do?' said Gevrol.

'It is quite straightforward sir,' said the Judge, 'I have given a good amount of my time to ruminating on the very subject and have come to the conclusion that we should recommend Commissaire Bassé and his deputy for a medal of valour, or some such.'

'Really?' spluttered Gevrol.

'Of course, sir, for their brave apprehension of the murderer and recovery of the money stolen from his victim, the Monsieur Sabat.'

'And what of the others?'

'Others sir?'

'Yes, yes, this list of names that the hotel fellow admitted to,' said Gevrol, 'what about them?'

'The ravings of a lunatic sir, driven insane by an unrequited and sinful,' Tanquerel paused, 'not to say depraved lust for the Corsican brute.'

'Really? But what about a trial?'

'My dear Mayor,' shrugged the Judge, 'I am having my physician draw up a document as we speak, confirming the certain lunatic tendencies, the hallucinations and delusions suffered by this poor gentleman. I fear the strain has quite deranged the fellow.'

'Deranged?' snapped Gevrol.

'Yes sir, the man was being blackmailed by the wicked and ruthless killer to provide rich pickings in the form of Sabat,' Tanquerel stood and drew again on his pipe, enjoying the moment and aware he was spinning it as far as he could, 'Indeed, I might fancy that this entire episode has little to do with our dear city.'

'How do you work that out Judge?'

'As I have already said, I have given a great deal of thought to this and have arrived at a beneficial conclusion sir.'

'I am all ears, Judge.'

'Well, you know what Corsicans are like, eh? They are not the sort to let something lie, and Sabat was a Marsellaise, a city famed for its links to the bandit isle.' A thick plume of smoke erupted from Tanquerel's nostrils, 'I would have to say that it has to be more than a coincidence.'

'You are saying that Loparelli deliberately went after Sabat?'

'Of course, nothing more to it. The rest are the ravings of a madman who will spend the rest of his days in the asylum.'

'Brilliant,' Gevrol clapped his hands, 'no trial?'

'Pointless,' said the Judge, 'it would be a pathetic sideshow with a very sick man as entertainment.'

'So, it's all over then?'

'Yes, sir.'

'Then will you come and eat with us on Sunday after Mass?'

'I would be delighted.'

The two men shook hands across the Mayoral desk. The Judge scooped up the dossier and headed for the door where he could see his man Rabuteau waiting for him.

'I have the physician's report sir,' said Rabuteau.

'Good man,' said the Judge, 'did you read it?'

'I did sir, I think you will find it satisfactory.'

'Thank you,' the Judge took the document and put it with the case dossier, 'now for the rest of the paperwork.'

'No trial?' asked Rabuteau.

Tanquerel said nothing but simply winked.

*

'I hear Nolet took responsibility for all of them,' said Mistretta, 'he said he and his man took care of Damozanne too.'

'The Butcher of Lille? The man truly is either mad or a genius,' Loup's lips twitched. It could have been the start of a smile. Mistretta watched carefully. He did not want to make it obvious.

'There will not be a trial. Nolet has been confirmed insane and will be sent away somewhere, to the Alps, I heard,' Mistretta rubbed his hands together, 'and by all accounts, our new commissaire is beside himself with fury.'

Another twitch, a fang bared.

'And to rub it in Boss, they're going to give Bassé a medal.'

That did it, Loup cracked a grin that bared all of his teeth, the natural, and the paid-for.

'Perfect,' said Loup, 'our Judge Tanquerel is a genius. I knew he would not let me down.'

'I have a case of Calvados prepared, sir,' said Mistretta, 'would you like to add anything else?'

'Of course,' if the grin were to get any bigger then Loup's head might split in two, 'send the dear Judge an entire roast boar.'

Loup's shoulders began to shake with mirth and before long he was gasping for air.

*

'Well, I heard that the man the chief shot was some villain up from Corsica with a beef to settle,' said Wimereux, 'and how do we know there's not another one on his way to avenge him?'

'You read too many soppy stories you do,' said Desnier, 'no-one is coming all this way for some scallywag on the run for looking the wrong way at someone's sister.'

'What?' said Wimereux.

'That's what they're like down there,' said Desnier.

'Wasn't Napoleon from Corsica?' said Wimereux.

'Yes, and ever since he came along, I reckon they think they're better than the rest of us,' said Desnier.

'Do you know many of them?' said Wimereux.

'Who?' said Desnier.

'Corsicans?' said Wimereux.

'Don't think so,' said Desnier, 'can't say I ever remember meeting one of them.'

'Then how do you know so much about them?' said Wimereux.

'It's common knowledge Wims,' said Desnier.

'It's not that common if I didn't know anything about it.'

'But you do now though don't you?' said Desnier.

'I suppose so,' said Wimereux.

'Well, there you go then,' said Desnier.

'We're safe from reprisals?' said Wimereux.

'Safe as houses mate, now where's that cup of coffee? My hands are going numb,' said Desnier.

'Just coming,' said Wimereux.

*

Jean-Luc Reynard was probably my second-best friend when I was a boy. Now he has been promoted. I shook his hand at the front door of the old house. Yes, it had been my parent's house, but today it was mine and Reynard was going to help me make some changes, some much-needed changes.

The top room, clogged with all the old memorabilia, the tools of the magician's trade, and the peculiar half-finished inventions, would be cleared out to the barn in the rear courtyard. Jean-Luc and his boys would whitewash all the walls and service the windows and doors.

Between the house proper and my quarters, there would be new lockable doors to divide the property. I planned to occupy the smaller tower wing, making use of the courtyard for access. It was big enough for one man to live quietly in a private manner. A luxury I had not been able to afford before. The rest of the house, the main part of the building with the modern kitchen, light salon with its big windows, and the bedrooms I would let out. I had a tenant in mind, and she arrived just ten minutes after Jean-Luc had left. I will admit that I was much more nervous when I saw her than I expected.

Marie was wearing black, as is the custom for a widow.

'Good afternoon, Marie,' I said, 'thank you for coming.'

'What is this about Stefan?' She came straight to the point, no anxiety, just positive concern. 'The rumours and the gossip are incredible. They say the papers are not telling the real story.'

'Come in, come in,' I took her elbow and guided her through the door, 'I have some coffee in the kitchen.'

Marie looked about the kitchen. 'It's nice to be back here,' she said, 'I always liked visiting your home.'

'Yes,' I said, 'I like it here.'

'What have you got to tell me?' That direct look, demanding answers.

I poured a coffee and passed her a cup.

'I do not know what you have heard Marie, but I am quite satisfied that Jean was killed by Loparelli, on behalf of Nolet, the concierge.'

'But they say he is raving mad?'

'He is,' I nodded, 'that is a certainty, and I did find him to be unreliable at first. However, I have spent some time considering the evidence and I have concluded his final confession was the most honest. I looked into the dossiers of the murders he claimed to have been a party to and found commonalities between enough of them to put it beyond doubt.'

Marie stared into her coffee cup, hoping perhaps to divine an answer.

'You are certain?' she said.

'I am,' I said, keeping my tone as even as I could, 'Jean's killer is dead, and his accomplice will never be a free man.'

'Good,' she took a sip of her coffee, 'and I am pleased that it was you who finished things.'

'I feel the same,' I said, 'to a degree.'

'What happens now?' she said, 'The case is closed, and the medal won before you have even settled back into the old house.'

'It has all happened so quickly,' I said, 'and while it is good to be back it is also true that we can never go back. I was here with Jean-Luc earlier, discussing the future.'

'Making some changes?'

'I am, yes. I have an idea or two about how this old house will be brought into use once more.'

'It is big for one man,' she smiled, 'you might get lost here.'

'I know,' I returned the smile, 'it is too big for me, so Jean-Luc is going to divide it up. I will have an apartment in the small tower wing with the separate staircase and servant's kitchen.'

'Cozy.'

'Yes, and the rest of the house,' I paused, 'I thought that perhaps you could see yourself and the children here?'

'Here?'

'Rather than in that rotting farmhouse near Vaucelles, so far from town and the schools.'

'Here?'

'Yes,' I said, 'I have thought about it a lot and it makes sense to me.'

'I don't know.'

'Take your time, think about it. Jean-Luc will take a few weeks to finish everything that needs to be done.'

'It's so much.'

'No Marie,' I said, 'as far as I am concerned it will never be enough. It is the least I can do for you, for Jean, for Elena and Guillaume. If it were the other way around Jean would have done the same for me.'

'He wouldn't, he was Jean.'

'Well, the offer is there,' I said, sipping the last of my coffee, 'think about it.'

'You would be living next door?'

'I don't have to,' I said, 'there is room at the barracks.'

'No. I would like it if you were close.'

'Neighbours?'

'Yes.'

My eyes burned with tears still unshed. I had to turn away and make a show of refilling the percolator for another pot of coffee.

If you enjoyed that adventure, here's a taste of what is coming next for the inspector.

Inspector Bassé and the Lost Boys

Prologue

Breathe, one, two, three, four, five, six.

I can hear my blood pounding in my ears. I'm beginning to feel the cold now. Air is sharp on the back of my throat.

There, just ahead, a woodsman's hut. No smoke. It must be empty.

In front of it is a grey shape. Motionless. No. I see its ribcage rise and fall imperceptibly. A wolf as big as a man, with a wound on its leg.

I wonder at its vulnerability. At mine.

I breathe, one, two, three, colder now.

The grey fur on the wolf is blurring. I blink at it as I creep past, push open the door to the moss and snow-covered hut.

Inside, it is dark, but there is a dry wood stack next to a pot-bellied stove. I open it up. It's kindled, ready to be lit. Tinder box on top.

I leave the door to the stove open for a minute to see what's here. A blanket, a cloak.

A growl or a moan takes my attention outside. The wolf is coming to.

I grab the cloak, wrap myself in it and take the blanket. I must bring the wolf inside, into the warm with me. I should be scared. Traditional knowledge says wolves, especially wounded beasts, are dangerous. Killers.

Somehow I am not afraid, but I don't know why.

Chapter One.

Nine Months Earlier, April 1889

Rain had been a constant companion for the weeks following the thaw. Umbrellas and overcoats colonised hallways, bringing souvenirs of the weather indoors with them. When it got to the point that I had become resigned to living the rest of my life underwater it suddenly stopped. Just like that.

I left the house in the morning and opened my umbrella and was shocked by the absence of rain drumming upon its fabric. I was still wading through puddles filled to the brim with muddy water, reflecting a sky that remained grey and threatening. I closed my umbrella but kept it with me, casting a wary eye at the charging cloudscape above.

The sky held onto its assorted cumulus, but in some parts, it had been scrubbed at by a giant hand to reveal a faint blue pigment that had not been seen for some time. I looked around and noticed one or two other townsfolk peering in perplexed fashion up above the rooftops as if they were trying to work out what it was that made today different from yesterday.

I was certain the change in the weather could only be a good thing, an omen of better times to come. A promise of fine weather would have a restorative effect on people's spirits.

But at the commissariat, the mood seemed low, as if it were still raining inside the building.

'Bonjour Sergeant,' I greeted Royer. He had just come on shift at the front desk and wore the look of a man craving his second coffee of the morning.

'Bonjour Inspector,' said Royer.

'Quiet night?'

'Tuesday nights are always quiet,' he said, 'much like the rest of the week at the moment.'

'Until market day?' I said.

'Until then, and no doubt if the weather stays dry,' he tapped the wooden desk for luck, 'we'll have a customer or two again.'

'Well, enjoy the peace while it lasts Sergeant,' I went past the desk and headed for my office where a quiet morning awaited, signing off papers and reviewing a report on a recent burglary.

*

Despite horror stories circulated about the detrimental effects of paperwork on an inspector's nervous system I have always found the work satisfying. Far worse is the requirement to redo paperwork not completed properly in the first instance. I had heard a story of an English King who signed his own death warrant. His chamberlain had made up the document to make a point to his highness. Not a career gamble to be recommended. Regardless of the tedium I found a quiet calm in the reading, checking, and signing off the pages that helped to build the edifice that is the state of France.

I had been thus engaged for an hour when Ouimet, my erstwhile Deputy Inspector and Sergeant Royer knocked on my door.

'Come in gentlemen,' it was my habit to keep my office door open, unless I was holding a meeting, or had something serious I needed to achieve, which would require all my powers of concentration.

'Good morning sir,' Ouimet came in and shook my hand, 'we had a report of a disturbance out on the Rue de Bouchers, so we sent a man out to take a look.'

'Might be serious sir,' said Royer, 'man with a gun and a hostage at the Langlois Notaire office.'

'Then the paperwork will have to wait,' I said, 'Let's go.'

'Ten minutes' walk from here,' said Royer, 'less for younger legs.'

'I have sent word to Doctor Richelieu's office,' said Ouimet, 'you never know.'

'Very sensible Ouimet,' I said.

*

The Langlois Notaire's office was a recent addition to the Rue de Bouchers and had seen a good deal of money spent on decoration and modernization while retaining a sense of old France. I'd noticed it a little while ago, but now, approaching it this morning in the crowded street I thought it looked a little out of place in our small, provincial city. It was the sort of establishment that may have been quite in keeping in Paris or Nantes, but I was not a businessman, so I should not judge these things.

As I drew closer, I could see our men were struggling with the crowd. Our first task was to help clear people away from the area. Men and women were shouting, demanding to know what was going on.

Sergeant Royer waded in. He had many years of experience in herding an unwilling public and he directed proceedings admirably. He pulled a police wagon across the road to block one side and cleared the other with his constables and his stentorian tones. Ouimet took a man with him to close off the rear of the building and ensure it was secure.

I approached the front of the building. Through the window I could see the lights were all on, illuminating the pale grey faces of a half-dozen terrified junior clerks. An older man had his back to the door. He held a shotgun in one hand and a revolver in the other. I remained still for a moment, taking in the fear in the clerk's eyes, the obvious strain in the shoulders of the old man. He was waiting for something. For someone to arrive perhaps. Maybe Langlois himself?

I tapped on the front door with the handle of my umbrella. The old man did not hear but the boys did, and their shock registered with the aged gunman. He turned slowly; his guns raised. I pushed open the door before I became aligned with his armaments.

'Good morning gentlemen,' I said cordially, 'I am Inspector Bassé and I understand there is a problem. An unhappy client.'

'A problem,' shouted the old man, 'there's a problem here alright. That thief, all dressed up as a Notaire, that thief should be swinging from the end of a rope for what he's done.'

'I don't doubt it, sir,' I said, 'and which one of these young men would you have me hang first?'

The old man lowered his guns, clearly worn out from the effort of maintaining such high emotion at his age. He was at the very end of his rope.

'That snake, Langlois has taken all my money, every last centime and I want it back.'

'Then why don't you ask him for it, monsieur?'

'I did. I have. He was going to pay me two weeks ago, but then he disappeared, and these lickspittle wretches will not tell me where he is, or when he will return.'

'Then I have news for you.'

'You do?'

'Indeed so,' I indicated his firearms, 'if you would be so kind as to put down your weapons first, Monsieur?'

'Bichot, David Bichot, is it good news?' The old man's face lit up with desperate hope, and for a moment I felt a little sympathy for his position. I would make this as painless as I could.

'I think so. I will bring you up to date in just a moment, but I do need you to surrender your guns.'

'What for?'

'Normal police procedure, sir. You will get them back.'

'Very well,' he bent down to put the guns on the floor, but halfway down he stopped with a grunt, 'my back.'

I stepped forward and took the guns from him and laid them on one of the desks out of his reach. Then I took both his hands and pulled them behind his back. A moment later he was handcuffed and had regained his former fury.

'What are you doing? I'm not the criminal here.'

'You are under arrest Monsieur Bichot.'

'But I am not the crook, it's Langlois that's the crook. You talk to him. You'll see.'

I gathered up his shotgun and revolver and marched him out through the front door of the shop. Ouimet and Leverrier were waiting in the street.

'Put him in the wagon and take him to the station house.'
Sergeant Leverrier took Bichot and walked him up the steps
into the wagon.

'We will talk together later, he and I. Ouimet, get in the
Notaire's office and take statements from the boys in there. I
want to know what's going on, why this old man lost his
temper?'

I called for Sergeant Royer.

'Yes sir?'

'Put these guns somewhere safe.'

'Yes sir,' said Royer, and he locked them in the box at the front
of the wagon.

'Where's that thief Langlois?' the old man spat through the
bars of the wagon door.

'Get him out of here,' I called to Leverrier, and the wagon
jerked and began moving off toward the commissariat.

'Excuse me, Inspector,' a white-haired gentleman called out
from across the street, 'actually, I would rather like to know
when the Notaire will be returning too?'

'Where is the Notaire?' called out another grey-bearded man.

'When we have news, we will let you know,' I said, 'if you have
a complaint, or you have any evidence that a crime has been
committed, then please visit the commissariat and speak to
our duty sergeant.'

There was a murmur of approval from the assembled
onlookers, and they turned away, going back to their business
now that the drama was concluded.

I followed Ouimet back into the Notaire's office. The clerks
were busy making coffee, and tidying papers, visibly relieved.
They were so young I wondered how long they had been out
of the schoolhouse.

'Good morning gentlemen,' I began, 'I am going to need
statements from all of you regarding this incident. Deputy
Inspector Ouimet will take them from you one at a time, but
before he does that, I would like to ask all of you two
questions. Raise your hand if you are able to answer.'

'Question one, where is your master, Notaire Langlois?'

I watched for the split-second looks, the silent coded messages the group used to communicate. I tried to read them. Not one of the boys raised a hand.

'Question two, when was the last time that the Notaire was here, in this office?'

Again, silence and the hands all stayed down. I picked out one of the boys nearest me.

'You lad, when was your master last in the office?'

'I don't know sir.'

'Two, three weeks ago?'

'I don't know sir.'

'Is anyone else having difficulties with their memory?'

More silence. Now the floor became most fascinating for them, and they hung their heads.

'Is it normal for Monsieur Langlois to be away for any length of time?'

Nothing.

'Ouimet, let us lock this office up. I think that a trip to the commissariat might loosen their tongues.'

I left the office and drew in a deep, chilly breath on the pavement. I shuddered. The weak sun was still not strong enough to make the icy breeze bearable. The crowd had dispersed. Nobody had suffered any injury. I had my doubts as to whether the guns were in a condition to fire, and whether or not they were loaded. I had further doubts that old Bichot had the physical strength to fire the shotgun at all.

One of the clerks concerned me. He had a look about him. Instinct told me more was going on than he was likely to let on. We would have to get them to the donjon and get them split up as soon as we could.

Leverrier returned with the wagon and Ouimet made sure the Notaire's office was secure while I elected to walk a longer route back to the commissariat. My objective was a visit with my old friend Jean-Luc Reynard, the master carpenter. Setting my shoulder to the wind as it began to pick up from the west, I set off.

Jean-Luc was, as ever, pleased to see me.

'Stefan,' he said, 'I have coffee on already. You must have picked up its scent.'

'Good timing,' I said.

'You are not here to arrest me then?'

'Why? Should I? Do you have a confession for me?'

'No, but I do confess I have everything you asked me for, to go in your house. It's all ready.'

'That is very good news Jean-Luc,' I said, 'except that now I get the bill for the renovations.'

Reynard had made new doors to divide the house between the rented part and my quarters. I had artisans working to ready the property through the last two weeks and now Reynard was ready too. The stars were aligning. In a week the house would be finished, and I could make good on a promise I had made.

'Your coffee Commissaire, and to accompany it some rather fine chocolate from a happy customer.'

'If only my customers would do the same,' I said.

'Well, you need to get better at arresting people.'

'What are you saying?'

'Or you need to be arresting a better class of criminal.'

'Stick to your woodwork, Jean-Luc.'

'I intend to,' he laughed, breaking off another piece of what was indeed, quite remarkable chocolate.

Available in most formats from good bookshops everywhere.

Other books coming soon in the series:

Inspector Bassé and the Heatwave
Inspector Bassé and the Revenant
Inspector Bassé and the Long Shadow

Follow Simon online, at Goodreads, Ko-Fi, Wordpress, Amazon, Threads, Instagram, Facebook, X and BlueSky